LUV.NET

LUV.NET

Bharti Mohan

PARTRIDGE

A Penguin Random House Company

To order additional copies of this book, contact
Partridge India
000 800 10062 62
orders.india@partridgepublishing.com

www.partridgepublishing.com/india

CONTENTS

Prologue..7

Part I 9

1 Junglecat 11
2 Lionking 22
3 The Past.. 35
4 Girl Without Panties... 46
5 The Realist.. 55
6 Friendship.. 61
7 The New Year 74
8 One-Sided Love 81
9 The Cobweb 100
10 Green Ideas Society... 111
11 Junglecat In Love 115
12 Junglecat Trapped 125
13 Junglecat Commits Suicide 131
14 Lionking Killed.. 137

Part II.. 143

15 Rebirth 145
16 Meeta And Abhi.. 156
17 Sex Experiences... 164
18 The Boyfriend.. 170
19 First Meeting 192
20 The Girlfriend 200
21 The Breakups... 210
22 Joining Broken Hearts... 222
23 Lionking In Love 230
24 Junglecat's Love.. 245
25 The Approvals.. 255
26 The Engagement.. 262
27 The Wedding.. 267
28 The First Night 272

Epilogue.. 275

PROLOGUE

A few years back, I was travelling from New Delhi to Chandigarh by Shatabdi Express. On the adjacent seat was seated a beautiful young girl. From the moment she took the seat, she was continuously tapping the keypad of her mobile phone with her nail. It took me sometime to understand that she was chatting with somebody through SMS. On the other side must be her boyfriend because the chatting continued till the train reached Chandigarh.

During the journey and afterwards, I kept on wondering what they were chatting about. That gave me the idea for this book.

The book is set in the year 2002 when Internet and Internet chatting was quite new in India and the chatting language was not that complex as it is today. I have used very simple Internet chatting language so that everybody is able to understand.

The purpose of the book is to enlighten the readers about the pitfalls of Internet chatting. One must exercise utmost caution in selection of chatting sites and the rooms they enter for chatting. Utmost care and discretion should be exercised in disclosing personal information on the Internet.

The other purpose is to encourage youngsters to make use of the Internet not only to acquire knowledge but to create a network of acquaintances and friends. A recent survey has shown that every year about 3,00,000 users are successful in finding their soul mates through the Internet. Maybe this year, you will be one of them.

My thanks to the unknown young girl who provided the idea for writing this book. My thanks to Mr Dhiraj (Dheeru) who was once a close Internet friend and instrumental in writing this book but was lost in the jungles of Yahoo. My thanks to Internet Explorer and Google which helped in searching the Internet for jokes, riddles, and puzzles which are reproduced in this book. And above all, my sincere thanks to Yahoo Messenger for being a part of this book.

The book is dedicated to all those who have found their life partners in the chat rooms on the Internet.

PART I

1

JUNGLECAT

Sunday, 23 December 2001

It was a Sunday morning, and as was the routine for sunny Sundays during winters, I was sitting on the back lawn of our house, basking in the warmth of the sun, sipping the cup of morning tea, and scanning the Sunday newspapers. But that Sunday was special as only the day before I had finished my semester exams, and that Sunday was the first holiday of winter break.

Soon Papa also joined me, and he also busied himself in the newspapers. Sonali usually gets up late on Sundays, and further, she was also on winter break, so nobody dared to wake her up. Mom also joined after sometime and asked whether she should serve the breakfast. So now it was time to wake up Sonali. I had also built up the natural pressure, so I left for my room. On the way to my room, I knocked at Sonali's door and told her to go down as Mom and Papa were waiting for breakfast. Sonali is my younger sister, very naughty and hot-tempered.

I refreshed myself and rushed downstairs for breakfast, as suddenly I felt very hungry. Mom had made Sunday special breakfast of aloo puri (potato curry and fried Indian bread) and aloo gobi stuffed parathas (Indian bread stuffed with potatoes and cauliflower) with curd and pickles. Everybody enjoyed the breakfast.

Suddenly Papa asked, 'Ashu, what is your schedule during the holidays?'

'Nothing special, Papa. But we were hoping you will be taking us out somewhere for a few days,' I replied, expecting Sonali and Mom to join in.

'Yes, Papa, let us go to Goa,' said Sonali.

'No, not Goa. It smells of rotten fish,' Mom objected.

'I think we should go to Shimla. It might snow during our stay,' I asserted.

'Yes, I have never seen snowfall,' Sonali seconded my proposal.

Mom again objected, 'But it will be too cold there, and you know I am prone to catching cold very easily.'

'Mom, please,' both me and Sonali pleaded at the same time.

'Nobody is asking me about my schedule,' Papa interfered.

'Sorry, Papa. What do you say?' I looked at Papa hopefully.

'OK. Shimla is final. But not this week. Next week I also have some office work at Shimla, so we shall go next week,' Papa agreed.

'Papa, let us go for New Year,' said Sonali.

'Dear, it is too crowded at the time of New Year. So we shall go after that,' said Papa.

'Sonali, Papa is right. We shall go after New Year. We shall celebrate New Year here,' I tried to reason with Sonali. She did not say anything. So it was decided.

'Ashu, should I apply some oil in your hair?' Mom asked.

'Sure, Mom,' I replied. I relished her light massage. This was like a lullaby, and sometimes I really fell asleep while she applied oil in my hair. Sonali never agreed for this; she did not like oil being applied to her hair. Mom reminded me not to wash my hair for half an hour. After relaxing there for some time, I left for my room to take a bath. It was too cold in the room, so after washing my hair and taking a bath, I switched on the hot-air blower.

With no burden of studies and nothing else to do, I decided to try my hand at Internet chatting. I switched on the computer and sat down comfortably in a chair at my study table. I had recently acquired Internet connection and was in the process of learning how to use it. With help from friends, I had learnt a few things like creating an email account, sending and receiving emails, searching on Yahoo, and a little bit of chatting on Yahoo Messenger. I had created an account on Yahoo Messenger. Yesterday night, I tried a few chat rooms but got a very cold response, and the chatting was not at all enjoyable. But my friends had always been discussing their experiences about chatting with lots of enthusiasm. Maybe something was missing somewhere. So I decided to give it another try. Maybe my ID sounded boring. So I decided to change it.

I started Internet Explorer, and the Yahoo page opened. I clicked on the Mail icon. As the mail page opened, I clicked on the Sign Up icon and began the process of creating a new email account. It asked for picking a Yahoo ID, and after a brief thought, I typed JUNGLECAT and checked the availability. It was available, and I filled in the other details and clicked on Create My Account. Immediately I got a new email ID. Then I logged on to Yahoo Messenger using my new ID, JUNGLECAT.

There were a number of chat rooms, but I knew what I was looking for. Immediately I clicked on Indian Rooms. A new lobby opened, and there were all sorts of rooms—Social Lounge, Business Lounge, Politics Lounge, Friendship Lounge, and many more—but I clicked on Flirt Chat and was immediately transported into a new room.

Suddenly there was a flood of messages from the guys present there. It seemed everybody there wanted to chat with me. I was at a loss which one to reply to. Randomly I replied to the guy nicknamed Janoo_675.

Janoo_675: hi. how are you?

JUNGLECAT: Fine and you?

Janoo_675: a/s/l?

JUNGLECAT: What?

Janoo_675: r u new here, I mean to chatting.

JUNGLECAT: Yes.

Janoo_675: oh. It means—age, sex, location.

JUNGLECAT: Don't u think it is rude to ask a lady about her age. Incidentally, that also answers your 2nd question i.e. sex.

Janoo_675: sorry about that. and your location?

JUNGLECAT: That I can't tell u now.

Janoo_675 : ok, accepted. your good name miss?

JUNGLECAT: Junglee.

Janoo_675: no jokes. please tell me your real name.

JUNGLECAT: Junglee. Both real as well as imaginary. Does it make any difference?

Janoo_675: not really. ok. what r u looking for?

JUNGLECAT: Nothing particular. May be some fun.

Janoo_675: really. I am also here for some real fun. r u ready to play the game.

JUNGLECAT: Game? What game?

Janoo_675: the sex game.

JUNGLECAT: How?

Janoo_675: u take off your clothes, and u keep on doing what I tell u.

JUNGLECAT: Hey you are not my master to order me like that.

Janoo_675: I am sorry. but how we will do sex if u dont take off your clothes.

JUNGLECAT: Did I say I wanted to have sex with you. You boys r all same, dirty minds, full of sex and only sex. Get lost. Bye.

Janoo_675: I am sorry. ok. bye. c u.

JUNGLECAT : Not me. Good bye.

The messages kept on pouring from naughty_guy, nude_guy, hot_boy, wild_in-bed, I_LUV_U, and many more. Some of these IDs were really outrageous and vulgar. I decided to try a few more. It was definitely interesting and enjoyable. I clicked on shekhar4u.

shekhar4u: hi

JUNGLECAT: hi

shekhar4u: how old r u

JUNGLECAT: 20

shekhar4u: I am 46. would u like to continue

JUNGLECAT: May be. Depends on what u want.

shekhar4u: I am very experienced and can teach u a few things

JUNGLECAT: like

shekhar4u: Best positions for sex

JUNGLECAT: That I can learn from KAMASUTRA. I don't need a person of my father's age.

shekhar4u: but we can do the practical here.

JUNGLECAT: You better go to some sex lab. Bye.

shekhar4u: bye

Immediately I got a message from I_LUV_U.

I_LUV_U: hello miss

JUNGLECAT: hello. a/s/l.

I_LUV_U : 22/m/Mumbai.

I said to myself, 'Come on, JUNGLECAT, you are learning fast.'

JUNGLECAT : What r u doing?

I_LUV_U : student. final year engineering. Computer Science and u?.

JUNGLECAT: MBA. Ist year.

I_LUV_U: and where do u live?

JUNGLECAT: In the jungle. what r u looking for?

I_LUV_U: a decent girl to make love to.

JUNGLECAT: love or sex?

I_LUV_U: both.

JUNGLECAT: Do u have any experience?

I_LUV_U: oh yes, lot of. u will see when I make love to you.

JUNGLECAT: Did I say I am game for that.

I_LUV_U: then why r u here. now come on. It is only imagination. I wont harm u.

JUNGLECAT: But I can. I have long nails and sharp teeth.

I_LUV_U: just tell me r u ready for sex or not?

JUNGLECAT : noooooooooooooooo.

I_LUV_U: then go find someone else. Bye.

Never mind. There were so many other guys who were still sending me all sorts of messages. One said, 'I am your slave.' I was amazed to find how low these guys can go just to have some sex talk with a girl. Next message was a surprise, as it was from a girl.

HOT & HUNGRY: hello there

JUNGLECAT: a/s/l

HOT & HUNGRY: 19/f/India

JUNGLECAT: Oh. so u r a girl. a student.

HOT & HUNGRY: yes. college.

JUNGLECAT: Ok. I am also a female.

HOT & HUNGRY: I know.

JUNGLECAT: What r u wearing?

HOT & HUNGRY: salwar kameej [an Indian dress].

JUNGLECAT: Which color?

HOT & HUNGRY: salwar is black and kameej maroon with low cut neck. my cleavage is clearly visible.

JUNGLECAT: That is nice. do you always wear such sexy clothes.

HOT & HUNGRY: yes and more than that I sometimes even don't wear a bra.

JUNGLECAT: Then we can't blame the guys.

HOT & HUNGRY: look JUNGLECAT I am not here to discuss fashion. I am looking for some action.

JUNGLECAT: Then go and find some hot and sexy guy.

HOT & HUNGRY: can u recommend somebody.

JUNGLECAT: You can try I_LUV_U

HOT & HUNGRY: thx.

And she went after I_LUV_U.

This fellow, sincerely yours, had been bothering me for quite some time.

JUNGLECAT: Are you sincerely mine?

Sincerely yours: oh yes miss. I am all yours.

JUNGLECAT : junglee billi hoon, katcha kha jaoongi [I am a wild cat, I will eat you without cooking].

Sincerely yours: i am ready madam. what should I offer first?

JUNGLECAT: it is your choice.

Sincerely yours: madam why don't u try my xxxxx; it is very tasty.

JUNGLECAT: Sure. What will u do the rest of your life? Join eunuch party.

Sincerely yours: u r making fun of me.

JUNGLECAT: How do u know it is very tasty. Do u really have such a flexible body to try it yourself?

Sincerely yours: u r impossible. bye.

JUNGLECAT: hahahahaha. bye.

I felt sorry for the guy. I should not have done that. But he came to the point too soon. Anyway let me try someone else. Let me see this one.

Suresh_lallu: hi JUNGLECAT

JUNGLECAT: Hi lallu

Suresh_lallu: humm

JUNGLECAT: How r u?

Suresh_lallu: I am fine. how r u ? I am here to learn something.

JUNGLECAT : What something?

Suresh_lallu: sex. I hope u don't mind.

JUNGLECAT: Mind what?

Suresh_lallu: teaching me

JUNGLECAT: Tell your papa to hire a tutor for u.

Suresh_lallu: no I cant tell papa. I want to have sex.

JUNGLECAT: How old r u?

Suresh_lallu: 17

JUNGLECAT: Then how come you are here. You are not an adult. Leave immediately or I will complain.

Suresh_lallu: no madam. Pl don't complain I am leaving.

He was really a *lallu* [naive].

But then I noticed that that there was a message from Sincerely yours on the lobby message board which said, 'JUNGLECAT is very rude. Don't go near her. She is very insulting.' Good, I was gaining popularity. After this, I started getting many times more messages. But I chose to click on HOT_GUY.

JUNGLECAT: Hi hottie

No response. I waited a minute, and there he was.

HOT_GUY: pl wait for a minute. let me bid good bye to the other girl.

JUNGLECAT: Ok.

And he was there before the minute expired.

HOT_GUY: hi. r u really rude?

JUNGLECAT: Judge yourself. Your location pl. Ok leave it; it does not make any diff.

HOT_GUY: I am from Nagpur. and u?

JUNGLECAT: I said it does not make any difference. I am an MBA student. You?

HOT_GUY: me too. what r u wearing?

JUNGLECAT: Jeans, shirt and sweater.

HOT_GUY: and underneath.

JUNGLECAT: Bra and panties.

HOT_GUY: which color?

JUNGLECAT: Black. Why?

HOT_GUY: I want to imagine how u will look in bra and panties.

'Ashu, lunch is ready. Come down. Your Papa is waiting.' It was mom calling for lunch.

'But, Mom, I just had breakfast.'

'Ashu, it is 1.30, and you had breakfast three hours ago.'

I looked at the clock. Oh my god. I did not realize I was chatting for three hours.

'OK, Mom. Coming in five minutes.'

HOT_GUY: r u there?

JUNGLECAT: Yes. mom called for lunch.

HOT_GUY: so let us do it fast. u take off your clothes. Ok. I have also taken off my trousers. I am holding your......

But before he could finish, I logged off. They were all alike. They all wanted to get into the panties of a girl as soon as possible. But it was good experience and time pass. I switched off the computer and rushed downstairs for lunch. After lunch I retired to my bedroom for a Sunday special siesta.

2

LIONKING

I woke up at 5 p.m. and went downstairs for a cup of tea. As Mom and Papa had gone out for some shopping, I called my younger sister, Sonali, to make me a cup of tea.

'Why don't you make it yourself?' replied Sonali.

'Sonali, please,' I again requested her. 'OK let us both make it.'

And she agreed. I was just standing there, and she made tea for both of us. We were sitting in the family lounge, sipping tea, when she asked, 'You were chatting on the net. Did you find anybody of your match?'

I was surprised by her knowledge. 'So you also do the chatting. Take care, this can be very dirty. But I am sure you are wise enough to do the right type of chatting. As to your question, no, I have not yet found anybody who is interesting enough.'

At that very moment, the doorbell rang, and Sonali opened the door. Mom and Papa had returned from the market with bags of groceries.

We sat there for some time watching TV. But there was nothing interesting, so I got up and went to my room. I picked up a book of economics and started scanning it. But my mind was not there. Then I picked up a fashion magazine and started turning the pages, but I found nothing interesting. So I turned on the computer and logged in to Yahoo Messenger and waited for the messages to pour in. I did not have to wait long, and I got an SMS from LIONKING007.

LIONKING007: hi catty

JUNGLECAT: Hi jungle ke raja [king of the forest]

LIONKING007: how r u this evening?

JUNGLECAT: Enjoying and you?

LIONKING007: fine. what is your name miss?

JUNGLECAT: What is there in a name. U can call me junglee.

LIONKING007: what is your real name?

JUNGLECAT: For the time being Junglee will be ok Mr. LION.

LIONKING007: no problem junglee. what r u looking for this evening?

JUNGLECAT: When LIONKING is there I can't hope to get much. What about U?

LIONKING007: today I am not hungry. yesterday I had a full meal. so today I just want some fun.

JUNGLECAT: What sort of fun?

LIONKING007: anything which will make me happy. some interesting and refreshing chatting.

JUNGLECAT: It is quite cold in this part of the country where I live.

LIONKING007: where do u live?

JUNGLECAT: In the jungles of northern India. and u?

LIONKING007: same. never seen u before.

JUNGLECAT: I am new in this forest and learning to find my way.

LIONKING007: good. be careful. this forest is full of harmful animals.

JUNGLECAT: Don't worry. I can guard myself. I have long nails and sharp teeth.

LIONKING007: oh really. then I will have to be careful.

JUNGLECAT: You better be if you want to have a refreshing evening.

LIONKING007: what do u do? I mean your profession?

JUNGLECAT: I am an MBA Ist year student. and you?

LIONKING007: same as u. where?

JUNGLECAT: Very clever. I will tell u later when the time comes. I won't ask u the same question. not now.

LIONKING007: I am in Delhi.

JUNGLECAT: Ok.

There was no message from him for two to three minutes. Perhaps he was disconnected. I buzzed him.

JUNGLECAT: Are you there?

Again no reply. Maybe he was the same type as others and got bored with all the meaningless dialogue and have left without even saying goodbye.

LIONKING007: junglee u still there?

JUNGLECAT: Yes. I was about to sign off. Thought u were like other guys. And got bored with our useless chatting.

LIONKING007: what do u mean by like other guys?

JUNGLECAT: All the guys here r interested only in sex. They want to get into your panties at the first instance.

LIONKING007: that is not solely their fault. once a girl enters this lobby she is game.

JUNGLECAT: But this lobby is for flirting and as far as I understand flirting does not necessarily mean having sex.

LIONKING007: u r right. flirting means charming the other person but your intensions can be good or bad.

JUNGLECAT: But intensions come afterwards, first charming. Anyway we r here for fun, so let us enjoy.

LIONKING007: what r u wearing?

I thought after all the sweet talk the bastard was coming to the same thing—sex.

JUNGLECAT: why?

LIONKING007: there is nothing in that. just tell me.

JUNGLECAT: Jeans, shirt and sweater?

LIONKING007: which color sweater?

JUNGLECAT: You guess?

LIONKING007: black

JUNGLECAT: You are right.

LIONKING007: and underneath?

JUNGLECAT: Bra and panties.

LIONKING007: let me guess the color. It is white.

JUNGLECAT: Right.

LIONKING007: junglee u know I have a friend here on the net. her name is Ruby. she goes to office without wearing a panty.

JUNGLECAT: She told u that. You must be very close to her.

LIONKING007: yes. we have spent a lot of time together. she is very sexy.

JUNGLECAT: She must be. does she wear a bra?

LIONKING007: I must not be telling u all these private things. but I don't know why I want to trust u.

JUNGLECAT: Thanks. do u have cyber sex with her?

LIONKING007: oh yes. so many times. she is very good.

JUNGLECAT: and experienced too.

LIONKING007: I will introduce u to her.

JUNGLECAT: No I don't want to.

LIONKING007: junglee don't be jealous. she is really high class.

JUNGLECAT: High class my foot. have u ever smelled her jeans. She must be smelling like a rotten fish without those panties down there.

LIONKING007: lol.

JUNGLECAT: lol?

LIONKING007: don't know. ok. u r new to the chatting. It means "laughing out loud".

JUNGLECAT: lol

JUNGLECAT: with how many girls are you friendly, LION?

LIONKING007: frankly so many. but Ruby is my favorite.

JUNGLECAT: LEAVE HER OUT OTHERWISE I LEAVE.

LIONKING007: ok babe. but pl don't shout.

JUNGLECAT: I am not shouting.

LIONKING007: on the net any text in capital letters means shouting.

JUNGLECAT: I am sorry. I was just emphasizing. that is why u r typing everything in lower case.

LIONKING007: no problem. u will learn everything very fast.

JUNGLECAT: everything? what do u mean?

LIONKING007: nothing. don't be too suspicious. I am a very straight forward person and I am not afraid of your sharp nails and teeth. lol.

JUNGLECAT: lol.

LIONKING007: what else have u learnt?

JUNGLECAT: a/s/l means age/sex/location, r stands for 'are' and u stands for 'you'. Anything else I need to learn.

LIONKING007: 4 stands for 'for', c stands for 'see'.

JUNGLECAT: what r u wearing?

LIONKING007: jeans, tea shirt and high neck sweater. guess the color.

JUNGLECAT: blue. am I right?

LIONKING007: no it is grey. now do u accept my friendship.

JUNGLECAT: ok. we r friends. what is ur real name?

LIONKING007: KRISHAN KANT MALHOTRA. friends call me KK. and yours? If u please.

JUNGLECAT: ABHILASHA GUPTA. u can call me ASHU.

LIONKING007: nice and thank God. I had almost compromised on calling u Junglee forever.

JUNGLECAT: u can continue calling me Junglee if u like that more.

LIONKING007: no I will call u Ashu. I told u I am from Delhi. If u like u can tell me your location.

JUNGLECAT: not yet. u belong to Delhi or stay in a hostel?

LIONKING007: I belong to Delhi and stay at home. college is only 30 minutes drive on bike.

JUNGLECAT: u have a bike. which one?

LIONKING007: Hero Honda CBZ. how do u go to college.

JUNGLECAT: I have my own car, Maruti Zen. but sometimes I go by bus also.

LIONKING007: good. ur dad seems to be very rich.

JUNGLECAT: don't know what u mean by very rich. but yes my Dad is quite successful in his business.

LIONKING007: what sort of business.

JUNGLECAT: pharmaceuticals manufacturing.

LIONKING007: my Dad is in service, OBC bank.

JUNGLECAT: nice. his job must be transferable. that means u have lived in many cities.

LIONKING007: oh yes. in my memory we have lived in Ludhiana, Ahmedabad, Shimla, Nagpur, Kanpur.

JUNGLECAT: who else is there in your family?

LIONKING007: my Mom, she switches between being a housewife and a lecturer. but she works part time only in private academies, and I have a younger brother aged 16, studying in Xth standard. his name is Rajan. what about ur family?

JUNGLECAT: I told u about my Dad. my mother is a housewife. I have a younger sister, aged 17, studying in plus 2. she is very naughty. I love her very much.

LIONKING007: now we should be more comfortable as we know each other better.

JUNGLECAT: thats right. r u fond of movies?

LIONKING007: yes. I never miss a chance to go to movies.

JUNGLECAT: which is the last one u saw?

LIONKING007: Kabhi Khushi Kabhi Gam

JUNGLECAT: u liked it?

LIONKING007: yes, it is good family drama.

JUNGLECAT: any other?

LIONKING007: lagaan.

JUNGLECAT: how was it?

LIONKING007: it was very good. nice story, good acting, melodious songs and above all my favorite game cricket as back drop.

JUNGLECAT: I have also seen it twice. It is really good. do u play cricket?

LIONKING007: used to in my school days. now I only watch it on TV. but I am a very keen lover of the game. do u play any games?

JUNGLECAT: no I don't play any games. I am a very straight forward person.

LIONKING007: stupid. I mean sports.

JUNGLECAT: yes I play badminton but I don't get much time. whenever I am free in the evening I do go for a game. sometimes I go to gym.

LIONKING007: r u fatty?

JUNGLECAT: yes like a buffalo. I weigh 80 kg. r u disappointed?

LIONKING007: I know u r joking. u cant be fat.

JUNGLECAT: u will see when we meet.

LIONKING007: r we meeting?

JUNGLECAT: no idiot, not now. I said when we meet. how much do u weigh?

LIONKING007: 60 kg. I have maintained myself. I also go to gym thrice a week. but why do u go to gym?

JUNGLECAT: to keep in good shape.

LIONKING007: pakdi gayee na [you have been caught lying]. now tell me.

JUNGLECAT: ok. I am slim, shapely and tall.

LIONKING007: what is ur height?

JUNGLECAT: 5'4"

LIONKING007: complexion?

JUNGLECAT: fair

LIONKING007: vitals?

JUNGLECAT: 35/25/36. what about u?

LIONKING007: height 5'9", fair, athletic body.

JUNGLECAT: KK I am tired now. we have been chatting for more than 2 hours. see u tomorrow.

LIONKING007: cant it be today, after dinner. Just a few minutes. Just to bid good night.

JUNGLECAT: u r hard to refuse. c u. bye

LIONKING007: bye.

I switched off the computer and sat there reviewing the day's happenings. This guy, KRISHAN KANT looked to be a nice and decent guy who was intelligent, well behaved, and had a good sense of humour. I had started liking him as a friend.

It was 7 p.m. I went downstairs and sat down with the family to watch the TV show KBC (*Kaun Banega Crorepati—Who Will be a Millionaire*). Everybody in the family liked the show. It was entertaining and educative. Dinner was served in the family room as nobody wanted to miss the show.

The wonderful voice of Mr Amitabh Bachchan was resonating in the room. 'Your next question is for twenty-five lac rupees. Who wrote the novel *The Fountainhead* and here are your options. . .' Before he could finish, I replied Ayn Rand. Everybody asked how did I know. 'I have read the novel,' I replied. We finished the dinner while watching the TV. I got up and went outside for a small stroll on the lawns.

I returned to my room. It was 10.05 p.m. I switched on the desktop and logged in to YM. And lo, there he was.

LIONKING007: hi. u r late. I have been waiting 4 u.

JUNGLECAT: I said after dinner. perhaps u had early dinner.

LIONKING007: yes.

JUNGLECAT: which branch r u specializing?

LIONKING007: finance.

JUNGLECAT: what r ur elective subjects?.

LIONKING007: Strategic Management & Entrepreneurship

JUNGLECAT: what did u have 4 dinner?

LIONKING007: today was Sunday special, chicken curry with rice and roomali roti [very thin Indian bread].

JUNGLECAT: u cook non veg at home?

LIONKING007: yes. what about u? u like non veg?

JUNGLECAT: no. our family is vegetarian. but we do eat eggs.

LIONKING007: Ashu u know after chatting with u I felt very hot.

JUNGLECAT: really?

LIONKING007: and I had to release the heat. lol.

JUNGLECAT: lol. and where did u release it?

LIONKING007: in the bathroom; on the toilet seat.

JUNGLECAT: how often u do it?

LIONKING007: whenever I feel hot and have the opportunity. what about u? u also do it?

JUNGLECAT: yes. I do. every gal does it.

LIONKING007: nothing bad in it. how often?

JUNGLECAT: same as u. whenever I feel the urge.

LIONKING007: where do u do it?

JUNGLECAT: that is one of the advantages of being a woman. I can do it anywhere, any number of times. in the bed, in the bathroom and even in the classroom.

LIONKING007: which is ur favorite place to do it?

JUNGLECAT: bathroom. bcz there it is more enjoyable when u r fully naked.

LIONKING007: u said classroom?

JUNGLECAT: yes. once I did in the classroom.

LIONKING007: how is it possible?

JUNGLECAT: it was very cold. but I was feeling really hot bcz one of my friends had told me how she kissed her boy friend.

JUNGLECAT: that day I was wearing loose trousers. I put my hands in the trouser pockets to keep them warm. but to my surprise one of the pockets had a big hole and my hand went further and touched my private parts.

JUNGLECAT: It felt good and I started rubbing it slowly taking care that nobody notices my small movements inside my panties.

JUNGLECAT: I was already very hot and it was over very soon and it was a big one.

LIONKING007: oh my God. u r soooooooooooo sexy. I am feeling hot even without touching u.

JUNGLECAT: then go to the bathroom. lol

LIONKING007: don't tease me. I am really awful.

JUNGLECAT: then go. release urself. anyway I was about to bid good night.

LIONKING007: ok. bye and good night. sweet dreams.

JUNGLECAT: good night. c u.

LIONKING007: tomorrow what time?

JUNGLECAT: may be 11.00 am. but don't wait pl.

LIONKING007: ok. bye.

I logged off and switched off the computer and light. I was also feeling the heat, so I pulled over the blanket and relieved myself. I did not have to wait much for the sweet sleep to come.

3

THE PAST

24 December 2001

Because of holidays, I again had my breakfast outside while enjoying the warmth of the sun. That became a routine during the holidays.

Mom: How did you fare in the exams?

Me: Very good, Mom, as usual.

Mom: Have you met Sakshi one of these days?

Me: Yes, Mom. We met day before yesterday for a few minutes in the cafeteria.

Mom: How is she?

Me: Fine. Busy in her studies.

Sakshi is a cousin of mine and Mom's favourite among all the cousins.

After sometime I got up and went to my room. After refreshing myself and changing into warm casuals, I switched on the desktop as I had a date with my new friend LIONKING007. I logged in to YM, and there he was.

LIONKING007: hi. what is up today?

JUNGLECAT: I don't have anything which can get up.

LIONKING007: lol.

JUNGLECAT: rather I have something which goes down once a month. and today it is down.

LIONKING007: is it very uncomfortable?

JUNGLECAT: no. WHISPER takes care. u know this is one of the disadvantages of being a woman.

LIONKING007: but u have so many advantages.

JUNGLECAT: like?

LIONKING007: u can have multiple orgasms.

JUNGLECAT: r u jealous?

LIONKING007: yes.

JUNGLECAT: poor guy. but that is your choice.

LIONKING007: how?

JUNGLECAT: when God created the universe, he lined up all men on one side and all the ladies on the other and asked which of the species would like to pee standing up. all the men shouted, "we". "well then the ladies get multiple orgasms", said God.

LIONKING007: lol.

JUNGLECAT: while on multiple orgasms, u know there are 4 types of orgasms.

    1. The positive orgasm: "Oh, yes, yes, oh yes, yeeeessss!!"

    2. The negative orgasm: "Oh, no, no, oh noooooo!!!"

3. The religious orgasm: "Oh god, oh my god, oh gooooood!!!"

4. The fake orgasm: "Oh KK, oh KKkk".

LIONKING007: lol. how do u know all these things?

JUNGLECAT: internet dear.

LIONKING007: if u allow may I ask if u have any sex experience.

JUNGLECAT: ist u tell me.

LIONKING007: ladies ist.

JUNGLECAT: no. not in this case.

LIONKING007: u know about Ruby and there are others like her.

JUNGLECAT: no. not that. the real one.

LIONKING007: hum. well once when I was in college.

JUNGLECAT: and the girl.

LIONKING007: she was also in college, one year junior.

JUNGLECAT: oh. how did it happen?

LIONKING007: is it necessary to go into details?

JUNGLECAT: if u feel comfortable.

LIONKING007: the family lived in our neighborhood and the girl would often come to our house with an excuse to consult me for studies.

LIONKING007: she was very smart and perhaps was interested in sex or an affair with me.

LIONKING007: we would often sit in my room all alone. one day she came into my room without knocking. I was in the bathroom and she opened the bathroom door and peeped in. I was changing clothes and at that moment was totally naked.

JUNGLECAT: I wish I was in her place.

LIONKING007: i can show u any time u wish.

JUNGLECAT: then what happened.

LIONKING007: she started giggling and kept on standing there looking at me and I got excited. she came farther into the bathroom and came very near me.

LIONKING007: I grabbed her and kissed her. she also became hot and we made love on the bathroom floor.

JUNGLECAT: was she virgin.

LIONKING007: I don't know but there was no blood. now u tell me.

JUNGLECAT: if u believe me I am still a virgin.

LIONKING007: have u ever kissed? I mean adult kissing.

JUNGLECAT: yes. very recently when I was in B. Com final year.

LIONKING007: who was he?

JUNGLECAT: he was a class fellow. it happened during the new year party.

JUNGLECAT: we have been dancing and enjoying ourselves. Gurdev and Aditya took 2–3 shots of tequila and asked us gals to try it. Poonam took one. that encouraged me and I also took one. I was on fire.

JUNGLECAT: and started dancing with more vigor. while I was dancing with Aditya he pulled me closer and whispered in my ear "u are gorgeous. may I kiss u?".

JUNGLECAT: I don't know when and how I said yes. as the light went out, he pulled me and kissed me hard. I don't know what got into me, I slapped him.

JUNGLECAT: as the light came on, he was nowhere to be seen and nobody knew what happened in the darkness.

LIONKING007: u r impossible. then why did u say yes.

JUNGLECAT: perhaps under the influence of tequila.

LIONKING007: then why did u slap him. he was not at fault.

JUNGLECAT: may be bcz after the kiss he tried to touch my boobs.

LIONKING007: ok. then the bastard deserved it.

JUNGLECAT: r u jealous?

LIONKING007: may be yes. but I am afraid also.

JUNGLECAT: now u tell me about ur kissing experiences which I am sure are many.

LIONKING007: why do u think so. I am not a big flirt. my ist experience was when I was in school. I was in 12th and there was this teacher who taught us mathematics. she was very beautiful and sexy. I often eyed her. perhaps she knew it.

LIONKING007: her husband was in merchant navy and was away for long periods.

LIONKING007: one day she asked me to come to her house in the evening as she wanted me to do extra practice at sums as exams were near.

JUNGLECAT: then?

LIONKING007: I did not suspect anything. she was alone at home. her little baby was sleeping. after sometime she started asking me awkward questions.

JUNGLECAT: like?

LIONKING007: have u any affair? have u ever kissed a girl? do u have any sex experience? I was feeling very awkward. I was sitting in a chair. she bent down over me and first kissed me on the cheek and then on the lips. first lightly and then very hard.

LIONKING007: I had become very hot but then I realized what was coming next. so I ran out of her house.

LIONKING007: and went straight to my house and into the bathroom and released my heat.

JUNGLECAT: oh my God. poor guy. u had the opportunity which every boy of ur age waits for but u missed it. u thought she was taking advantage of u.

LIONKING007: u r right. I dont regret it. it would have been exploitation.

JUNGLECAT: I am proud of u 4 that.

LIONKING007: I myself feel the same.

LIONKING007: today I have to go to gym at 6.00 pm. so we may not meet in the evening.

JUNGLECAT: ok. I am also going to the gym today. we shall meet after dinner.

LIONKING007: ok. bye. Luv u.

JUNGLECAT: what?

LIONKING007: nothing. It is just a way of saying bye bye.

JUNGLECAT: bye. see u.

I logged off and sat there for some time thinking about him. How good he was at chatting. He seemed to be sincere and a thorough gentleman. He had not asked me even for a kiss so far. It looked like he was interested in true friendship and a lasting relationship. But I told myself to be careful and not to let it develop into a serious affair; for the time being, play along but to a limit.

After lunch, I took a nap. In the evening, I went to the gym. After dinner, I retired to my room and again logged in to YM to see what Mr LIONKING007 was up to. Immediately there was a flood of messages from the sex-hungry guys. But I was looking for LIONKING. He was not there, so I decided to play along with the other guys to gain some more experience in Internet chatting. LIONKING's sex partner Ruby_4_U was also there. For a moment, I thought of chatting with her but later rejected the idea because I was not sure whether LIONKING had told her about me and my ID. He may have. So I turned my attention to the messages I was receiving.

Madeforyou: hi there. mewww.

JUNGLECAT: mewww. hi. hi brother.

Madeforyou: no brother. I am ur friend. u can call me Sandy.

JUNGLECAT: ok sandy. a/s/l.

Madeforyou: 25/m/Hyderabad. u?

JUNGLECAT: 23/f/Hyderabad.

Madeforyou: very good. same city. If we become friends we can easily meet.

JUNGLECAT: humm.

Madeforyou: what do u say?

JUNGLECAT:?

Madeforyou: where r u lost?

JUNGLECAT: actually I am waiting for a friend. I think he is here. so pl excuse me. c u some other time. bye.

Madeforyou: bye. c u soon. remember my id.

LIONKING007: u still there. very sorry. i am late.

JUNGLECAT: just relax. it does not matter.

LIONKING007: how long have u been waiting?

JUNGLECAT: may be 30 minutes. but I killed my time by chatting with these stupid guys.

LIONKING007: u r so cool.

JUNGLECAT: u too. KK do u have a girl friend?

LIONKING007: yes. u.

JUNGLECAT: not me or Ruby. i mean in real life.

LIONKING007: not really. but an affair is just developing. I am not sure whether I can call her a girl friend.

JUNGLECAT: who is she?

LIONKING007: her name is Neelu. she is a class fellow.

JUNGLECAT: pl tell me in detail.

LIONKING007: nothing much in it. she is very beautiful & I like her very much. we have been just staring at each other. talked to each other a few times and have started exchanging notes.

JUNGLECAT: have u expressed ur feelings to her.

LIONKING007: no. I have not been able to gather the courage.

JUNGLECAT: coward. I am sure if u tell her u like her she is not going to slap u.

LIONKING007: I am afraid she may turn me down.

JUNGLECAT: no she cant. she cant turn down a nice guy like u. and u said she also seemed to be interested in u.

LIONKING007: may be u r right.

JUNGLECAT: then dont waste time. be a man. take her hand and say u luv her.

LIONKING007: u r not jealous?

JUNGLECAT: why should I be? I am just a new friend.

LIONKING007: u r more than that.

LIONKING007: do u have a boy friend?

JUNGLECAT: no.

LIONKING007: so I still have a chance of becoming ur boy friend.

JUNGLECAT: take ur chance. good luck.

LIONKING007: now tell me about ur past affairs.

JUNGLECAT: when I was in 12th standard, there was a boy named Jatin. He was very handsome and active in all school activities. I started liking him and he was also attracted to me bcz of my extrovert nature and would often eye me.

JUNGLECAT: once our class went on a picnic. we were to leave at 7.00 AM from the school. but bcz of rain I was delayed by a few minutes and when I boarded the bus it was full and the only empty seat was with Jatin.

JUNGLECAT: I happily occupied the seat and thanked the rain god for delaying me. we greeted each other with a smile.

JUNGLECAT: everybody was in a festive mood. it was announced that everybody will sing some song or tell a joke or do some mimicry.

JUNGLECAT: we were sitting in the front. so soon our turn came. Jatin sang a song baharo phool barsao mera mehboob aaya hai [oh spring, shower flowers, my beloved has come]. while singing he was eyeing me and I was red in the face and hot in the pants.

JUNGLECAT: next my turn came. i was telling Santa Banta joke when the bus gave a big jerk and I fell down upon Jatin. he held me and our bodies touched each other.

JUNGLECAT: he squeezed my hand and winked at me and immediately I had an orgasm. I could not complete the joke and said sorry.

JUNGLECAT: I sat there with my eyes looking down and feeling the warmth. I was really happy. but after that I could not meet his gaze. throughout the picnic I avoided his glare and nothing more happened.

LIONKING007: that was too sexy. and after that.

JUNGLECAT: we started meeting in the park in the evenings quite often. but that was very childish. one day somebody saw us and reported to my mother.

JUNGLECAT: mother ist tried to make me understand the repercussions of such an affair and then threatened to report the matter to my Dad.

JUNGLECAT: good sense returned to me sooner than later. no harm was done and I reconciled to the situation in a few days and stopped meeting the boy.

LIONKING007: so that is it. I am really hot Ashu.

JUNGLECAT: then what can I do? go relieve yourself.

LIONKING007: surely I will have to do that tonight.

JUNGLECAT: it is 11.30 and I think we should call it a day.

LIONKING007: just a few minutes more.

JUNGLECAT: these r holidays and we have got so many full days to ourselves.

LIONKING007: ok.

JUNGLECAT: further I am also feeling the heat. so good night and MERRY CHRISTMAS.

LIONKING007: MERRY CHRISTMAS. Good night and sweet dreams. c u.

JUNGLECAT: c u 10.00 AM. bye

LIONKING007: bye.

4

GIRL WITHOUT PANTIES

25 December 2001

Next morning I got up late as these were holidays, went downstairs, and asked for a cup of tea and started scanning the newspaper. As I was sipping tea, Sonali came and sat down next to me.

'Don't you think you are spending too much time on chatting?' she said in a very low voice.

'You know, every new thing has its charm for the first few days,' I replied in the same tone.

'These are holidays, and I was hoping that we will go to the movies today,' she complained.

'Sonali, there is no good movie showing this week.' I tried to put her off.

'That's an excuse. Actually you are more interested in chatting,' she raised her voice a bit.

'What is the matter?' asked Mom, entering the room.

'Mom, I was suggesting that we all should go to the movie today,' said Sonali as if to get Mom on her side.

'Both of you can go. I am going to the mandir in the evening. Some Mahatma Ji have come from Haridwar, and he is going to deliver a lecture on the relevance of Geeta in today's world,' Mom replied.

I was relieved a bit, but Sonali was adamant and I had to agree. It was decided that we shall go for the 6.30 p.m. show.

I immediately got up, asking Mom to prepare breakfast. I went to my room, refreshed, and called our servant Raju to bring the breakfast to my room.

I switched on the computer. It was eleven o'clock, so I was late by one hour. I did not know how Mr LIONKING would react. I logged in to YM and waited for him to appear. He was there in the list, but his SMS did not come. Maybe he was annoyed. There were numerous messages from other guys, but I was interested only in LIONKING. Maybe he was with his friend Ruby. I looked in the list, and Ruby_4_U was there. I clicked on LIONKING007 and sent a message saying I was waiting. His reply came immediately.

LIONKING007: so what? I have also waited for so long.

JUNGLECAT: sorry.

LIONKING007: I am with Ruby and she is not letting me go.

JUNGLECAT: ok. stay with her. I am going to find somebody else.

LIONKING007: just a minute. let me bid her bye bye. ok. good morning and Merry Christmas.

JUNGLECAT: Merry Christmas.

LIONKING007: hey. u have learnt quite fast, now u r inserting images.

JUNGLECAT: so u were with Ruby. must be relieved and cool now.

LIONKING007: lol. u r jealous.

JUNGLECAT: no. not at all. I was just wondering.

LIONKING007: wondering what?

JUNGLECAT: leave it yaar. did u enjoy with her.

LIONKING007: no it was Mahabharta [big fight] today.

JUNGLECAT: why?

LIONKING007: firstly she was furious why I was not replying to her SMS 4 the last 2 days.

LIONKING007: then I told her about u? that was like adding fuel to the fire. she was like a mad cow and shouting all sorts of obscenities at me.

JUNGLECAT: what did u tell her about me?

LIONKING007: just that I have made a new friend and that she was very nice and interesting. hearing this she started shouting, "THEN WHY R U HERE. GO, GO TO HER AND LICK HER. U R A SON OF A XXXXX," etc etc.

JUNGLECAT: do u think she loves u?

LIONKING007: loves my foot. she is a sex maniac. all the time she just wants sex. she is a dirty cheap lady.

JUNGLECAT: dont be so angry. she is ur friend.

LIONKING007: no longer. she even abused u. what right she has got to drag u into our fight.

JUNGLECAT: why did u bring me up before her?

LIONKING007: that was really stupid of me. I am sorry. but I will teach her a lesson.

JUNGLECAT: should I talk to her?

LIONKING007: no u should not meet her. she will insult u.

JUNGLECAT: but that day u were insisting on my meeting her.

LIONKING007: at that time I did not know how nice u were and how cheap she was.

JUNGLECAT: have u told her my id or my name?

LIONKING007: yes I have given her your id but not the real name.

JUNGLECAT: ok.

LIONKING007: what r u upto? u r not thinking of meeting her?

JUNGLECAT: I may be.

LIONKING007: but why. she has no class.

JUNGLECAT: what is she doing? u said she was serving somewhere.

LIONKING007: she is a receptionist in some medicines distribution company at Chandigarh.

JUNGLECAT: Chandigarh? what is such a dirty lady doing in such a beautiful city.

LIONKING007: forget her. let us talk about something else.

I did not reply for some time as if I was disconnected. He was continuously buzzing me. I immediately logged off and again logged in with my earlier ID ASHU_THE_GREAT.

I immediately sent an SMS to RUBY_4_U.

ASHU_THE_GREAT: hi. beautiful lady.

No reply.

ASHU_THE_GREAT: hi sweety. how r u?

No reply.

ASHU_THE_GREAT: hi sexy.

No reply.

ASHU_THE_GREAT: want to have sex?

Again no reply. May be she was busy with somebody else. But her status was showing her as idle. I tried again.

ASHU_THE_GREAT: 10" here.

No reply.

ASHU_THE_GREAT: I will take u to the 7th heaven.

RUBY_4_U: hi. a/s.

ASHU_THE_GREAT: 22/m. and u?

RUBY_4_U: 24/f. what is ur specialty.

ASHU_THE_GREAT: I am an all rounder. can do anything u ask for.

RUBY_4_U: oh really. then we shall have great time.

ASHU_THE_GREAT: I have noticed u r always online. what do u do?

RUBY_4_U: I am a receptionist and logged in full time.

ASHU_THE_GREAT: but today is a holiday. how come u r in the office?.

RUBY_4_U: I am doing overtime. I love chatting.

ASHU_THE_GREAT: chatting or?

RUBY_4_U: u r right. what is there in chatting only. I am more into it for sex.

ASHU_THE_GREAT: I am a great lover. by the way are u single or married?

RUBY_4_U: why do u ask that?

ASHU_THE_GREAT: no problem if u dont want to tell.

RUBY_4_U: I am married.

ASHU_THE_GREAT: then why r u seeking sex here? r u not satisfied with ur husband?

RUBY_4_U: why should I tell u all these details?

ASHU_THE_GREAT: ur choice. I just want to understand the lady before making luv to her. what is ur husband doing?

RUBY_4_U: he is a cashier in a bank.

ASHU_THE_GREAT: how old is he?

RUBY_4_U: 30. but he is totally naïve as far as sex is concerned.

ASHU_THE_GREAT: does not he make love to u?.

RUBY_4_U: not as often as I want. so I make love to him as and when I want.

ASHU_THE_GREAT: u mean u r the dominant partner.

RUBY_4_U: yes. that is why I am here all the time trying to learn newer methods and make it different every night.

ASHU_THE_GREAT: oh. that means u learn the theory here and do the practical with ur husband. he is your guinea pig. lol.

RUBY_4_U: lol.

ASHU_THE_GREAT: do u have any extra marital affair?.

RUBY_4_U: that I cant tell u.

ASHU_THE_GREAT: to be fair I should not have asked. sorry.

RUBY_4_U: no problem. yes I have with my boss.

ASHU_THE_GREAT: how often.

RUBY_4_U: once in a while. now come on.

ASHU_THE_GREAT: it means u r a bitch.

RUBY_4_U: what?

ASHU_THE_GREAT: I am ur husband. a lallu.

RUBY_4_U: no it cant be u?

ASHU_THE_GREAT: yes. I am not but could have been. here everybody is masked & cloaked. so be careful.

RUBY_4_U: then who r u?

ASHU_THE_GREAT: ask LIONKING007.

RUBY_4_U: JUNGLECAT?

ASHU_THE_GREAT: yes, u filthy slut.

RUBY_4_U: I will kill u.

ASHU_THE_GREAT: u better reflect on ur life. otherwise u r sure to be in big trouble someday. bye and good luck.

She was really a filthy whore, a sex maniac. I felt really sorry for her. I logged off and again logged in as JUNGLECAT.

Immediately I got an SMS from LIONKING007.

LIONKING007: where have u been?

JUNGLECAT: I had gone to meet ur good friend RUBY, the great sexy lady.

LIONKING007: oh no. I told u not to.

JUNGLECAT: but I had to. to know the real story.

LIONKING007: what do u mean?

JUNGLECAT: did u know she was married?.

LIONKING007: no.

JUNGLECAT: she is not satisfied with her husband and calls him a LALLU.

LIONKING007: really.

JUNGLECAT: did u know she has affair with her boss?

LIONKING007: really.

JUNGLECAT: yes. and whatever she does here she practices that on her husband. she uses him as a guinea pig.

LIONKING007: total filth. disgusting. I am ashamed of myself to have been involved with such a whore.

JUNGLECAT: now forget her and never go near her.

LIONKING007: u r right. thanks.

JUNGLECAT: u know me and Sonali r going for a movie in the evening.

LIONKING007: which one?

JUNGLECAT: I don't know. Sonali will decide. I think it will be either Harry Potter and the Philosopher's Stone or The Lord of the Rings.

LIONKING007: I hear The Lord of the Rings is good. Harry Potter is also ok if u r interested in that sort of stuff.

LIONKING007: then we will meet at 10.30 after dinner.

JUNGLECAT: ok. bye for now.

LIONKING007: bye. luv u.

5

THE REALIST

We came back from the movie at about 9.30 p.m. Dinner was ready, but I was not feeling hungry as we had some snacks during the interval. I had a hurried dinner and got up to retire to my room.

'How was the movie, Ashu?' Papa asked.

'It was OK. Sonali liked it very much. Actually Harry Potter is basically for children, but everybody likes it as it is very different and interesting. Both of us had read the book also,' I replied.

'Papa, you and Mom should also see it,' Sonali added.

'No, I am not interested in ghosts and magic. Such films are very frightening,' replied Mom, before Papa could say anything.

And everybody had a good laugh. I left for my room.

I changed into night clothes, switched on the hot-air blower, and sat down comfortably in the chair for a fresh session with LIONKING. Perhaps he was waiting for me because as soon as I logged in, immediately I got his SMS.

LIONKING007: hi darling.

JUNGLECAT: hi. so now u r progressing step by step. very clever.

LIONKING007: what do u mean?

JUNGLECAT: ist luv u and now darling.

LIONKING007: if u have objection, I wont call u that again.

JUNGLECAT: no I dont have any objection. but we have not come to that stage yet.

LIONKING007: how was the movie?

JUNGLECAT: it was ok, well made but the book is more interesting.

LIONKING007: I have also read the book but I don't believe in these things.

JUNGLECAT: when u were younger, ur grand mom or mom must have told u some fairy tales. how did u like them?

LIONKING007: they were quite interesting and I enjoyed them very much.

JUNGLECAT: so this Harry Potter story is also basically for children. It is another matter that people of all ages like it.

LIONKING007: but I cant believe the things and happenings mentioned in the story.

JUNGLECAT: look KK. it is all fiction. a set of conditions and circumstances have been created and u must view the whole story in the light of those circumstances. basically it is a story of victory of good over evil.

LIONKING007: but still?

JUNGLECAT: do u believe in RAMAYANA?

LIONKING007: yes.

JUNGLECAT: when Hanuman Ji [Hindu god] went in search of Mata Sita [wife of Lord Rama], how did he cross the ocean spanning 350 km?

LIONKING007: by flying over it.

JUNGLECAT: he was an animal not a bird?

LIONKING007: u cant compare Ramayana with Harry Potter.

JUNGLECAT: how could Hanuman travel a distance of 4800 km from Lanka to The Himalayas and back in a single night?

JUNGLECAT: what was his velocity? 100 km/h or 200 km/h or 400 km/h. Just imagine it.

LIONKING007: he was a God and could reach anywhere in no time.

JUNGLECAT: u mean 'apparate' in terminology of Harry Potter.

LIONKING007: do u mean Ramayana is also a fiction story.

JUNGLECAT: no I dont mean that. it is a story of victory of good over evil.

LIONKING007: u have very strong logic. do u believe in God?

JUNGLECAT: yes I do. I am not an atheist.

LIONKING007: do u go to mandir [Hindu temple]?

JUNGLECAT: no, if I have a choice.

LIONKING007: why?

JUNGLECAT: u go to mandir?

LIONKING007: yes.

JUNGLECAT: what for?

LIONKING007: to pay obeisance to God.

JUNGLECAT: u mean he lives in a temple. u must have a small mandir in your house also. why not say your prayers there. does the God live only in big temples?.

LIONKING007: but all the people go there.

JUNGLECAT: has anybody met the God there? people go there bcz offering a prayer to the stone statue of God gives them comfort and strength.

JUNGLECAT: otherwise God is everywhere; in every minute particle; inside u and me. why search Him outside. Just bend ur head down, close ur eyes and u will feel Him inside u.

LIONKING007: u r a philosopher yaar [friend].

JUNGLECAT: which temple u go to?

LIONKING007: Radha Krishna [Krishna is a Hindu god, and Radha was his beloved] temple. It is near our house.

JUNGLECAT: what do u think of the affair of Radha and Krishna?

LIONKING007: it was divine.

JUNGLECAT: have u ever wondered what happened to Radha after Krishna left Gokul for Mathura to kill His maternal uncle Kansh.

LIONKING007: no I don't know. do u?

JUNGLECAT: next time u go to the temple ask the priest. let us see how much he knows.

LIONKING007: ok. I will ask.

JUNGLECAT: have u ever gone to a Lord Shiva temple?

LIONKING007: yes, many times.

JUNGLECAT: then u must have seen females offering milk on the Shiva Lingam. what is that for? all that milk goes down the drain.

LIONKING007: I have also wondered why these ladies worship Shiva Lingam so lovingly.

JUNGLECAT: u know what is Shiva Lingam. it is sexual organ of Lord Shiva. and see how easily and fondly ladies refer to it. ask them to replace Shiva with their husband's name. no lady will do it.

LIONKING007: lol.

JUNGLECAT: in Hindu religion, a married woman considers her husband to be a God. then why not wash the Lingam of their husbands with milk.

LIONKING007: lol. u r being critical of our gods.

JUNGLECAT: no I am not at all critical of the gods. I am only criticizing the blind and illogical faith of the people. I am critical of our superstitious society.

LIONKING007: u r really a thinker. I salute u.

JUNGLECAT: KK it is too late. let us go to bed.

LIONKING007: u mean together. 😊

JUNGLECAT: no stupid, in different cities, houses, rooms and beds.

LIONKING007: 😶

JUNGLECAT: ok. good night.

LIONKING007: luv u. . . 😳 just a minute. I just sneezed. Just wait a few minutes and then leave.

JUNGLECAT: do u believe in these superstitions?

LIONKING007: sometimes I do believe.

JUNGLECAT: did u have hiccups last night?

LIONKING007: no. why?

JUNGLECAT: i was remembering u the whole night.

LIONKING007: there are many more such superstitions. some people say that if a cat crosses ur way, something bad will happen to u.

JUNGLECAT: and if u see an elephant while coming out of ur house, it is considered good.

LIONKING007: it is said that if u have itching in ur right palm, u r likely to receive money.

JUNGLECAT: and it is left hand 4 women. right eye twitching is good for men and left eye for women.

LIONKING007: do these superstitions have any meaning?

JUNGLECAT: some of them can be justified.

LIONKING007: then there is a superstition that cutting nails, shaving, stitching and sweeping at night is inauspicious.

JUNGLECAT: this can be justified. in olden days there was no electricity and performing these tasks in darkness could cause injuries.

LIONKING007: most of these superstitions r ridiculous.

JUNGLECAT: the most disturbing thing is that educated people like u still believe in these superstitions.

LIONKING007: no I dont.

JUNGLECAT: then why did u stop me from leaving after u sneezed.

LIONKING007: that was an excuse to chat with u a few minutes more.

JUNGLECAT: good night now.

LIONKING007: good night. luv u.

6

FRIENDSHIP

26 December 2001

Next day I was with college friends during the day. We had lunch together at a Chinese restaurant, and I came home quite late and was very tired. After having some light snacks and a glass of milk, I retired to my room, changed clothes, and snuggled into the blanket. I immediately fell asleep and woke up at nine o'clock. I refreshed myself and went down to have dinner.

I had not met LIONKING the whole day. He may have waited for me and must be annoyed with me. I switched on the desktop and settled into the chair for another session of chatting with the LIONKING. I logged in to YM, and there was a flood of messages as usual but no message from LIONKING. He was online and present in the lobby. So he was ignoring me to show his anger. I sent him an SMS.

JUNGLECAT: hi king of the jungle.

LIONKING007:

JUNGLECAT: cool down. I am really sorry, darling.

LIONKING007: say it again.

JUNGLECAT: darling

LIONKING007:. where were u? I am online since 5 o'clock.

JUNGLECAT: I was with college friends the whole day. when I came back I just lay down on the bed for a nap, but overslept and woke up at 9 o'clock only.

LIONKING007: u will have to pay some fine.

JUNGLECAT: I am ready. what?

LIONKING007: a kiss.

JUNGLECAT:

LIONKING007: a flying one yaar.

JUNGLECAT:

LIONKING007: puchhhhh. how sweet.

JUNGLECAT: now happy?

LIONKING007: overjoyed.

JUNGLECAT: just a moment. there is an SMS from Ruby.

JUNGLECAT: it just says very sorry and thank u.

LIONKING007: a few minutes ago I also recd a similar SMS. It said very sorry and thank u for JUNGLECAT. What does she mean?.

JUNGLECAT: it simply means she was sorry for her behavior and thanks I think are for showing her the right way.

LIONKING007: good 4 her. what r u wearing today?.

JUNGLECAT: night dress. pajamas and sweatshirt.

LIONKING007: grey color?.

JUNGLECAT: u have very sharp eyes. I should be careful while changing clothes.

LIONKING007: what is ur favorite dress; jeans or punjabi suit?.

JUNGLECAT: I am more comfortable in jeans.

LIONKING007: men don't have much choice. have u ever tried a sari [an Indian dress, about five metres long draped around the body in various styles]?

JUNGLECAT: no. I was too young to try that. but now someday I will try it.

LIONKING007: what kind of jewelry do u like, diamond or gold?

JUNGLECAT: r u planning to give me a gift. I will accept with thanks whatever u give me. but diamonds r 4 ever.

LIONKING007: lol. I wish I could send u a present but u have not given me ur address.

JUNGLECAT: not now. have patience.

LIONKING007: why do ladies luv jewelry so much?

JUNGLECAT: ladies r very wise. they know how to save 4 the future. Jewelry is their insurance 4 the future.

LIONKING007: and they know how to collect it. a lady was walking past a jewelry shop when she saw a diamond necklace in the show window which she really liked.

LIONKING007: she went inside and said to the sales lady "can u hold that necklace 4 a small deposit until my husband does something unforgivable".

JUNGLECAT: lol.

LIONKING007: what is ur favorite food?

JUNGLECAT: normally I eat Punjabi food at home. but when I dine outside I relish Italian.

LIONKING007: I like Muglai.

JUNGLECAT: muglai is mostly non veg?

LIONKING007: yes. chicken briyani is my favourite.

JUNGLECAT: do u drink?

LIONKING007: I don't even stand near the place where people r drinking. I just take a seat & sit there.

JUNGLECAT: lol. tell me.

LIONKING007: sometimes I take beer and at parties I do take a drink or two. do u drink?

JUNGLECAT: no yaar. u know what happened when I took that tequila shot.

LIONKING007: I have tried taquila once or twice. It gives u immediate kick.

JUNGLECAT: kick on the ass. lol.

LIONKING007: lol. do u like dancing?

JUNGLECAT: yes. I am mad for dancing. at parties I dance a lot. sometimes I close my room and play the audio system at high volume and dance alone.

LIONKING007: I am an awful dancer.

JUNGLECAT: what sort of music/songs u like?

LIONKING007: I like nearly anything, depending on my mood. but jazz and rock r my favourites. which is your favourite?

JUNGLECAT: Indian classical, ghazals [a type of poetry] and old hindi film songs. I like Manna Dey songs and Jagjit Singh ghazals.

LIONKING007: I am also a fan of Jagjit Singh Chitra Singh.

JUNGLECAT: which is ur favorite ghazal?

LIONKING007: "sarkati jaye hai rukh se nakaab ahista aahista" [the cover on the face is sliding down very slowly].

JUNGLECAT: r u trying to apply it to me?

LIONKING007: no I did not mean it but it incidentally fits u. now open up fast?

JUNGLECAT: open up?

LIONKING007: I am not asking u to open ur clothes?

JUNGLECAT: I thought u were.

LIONKING007: r u ready 4 that?

JUNGLECAT: I may be if u ask.

LIONKING007: ok. I am asking.

JUNGLECAT: will u do to me what u have been doing to Ruby?

LIONKING007: do u want me to do that?

JUNGLECAT: yes.

LIONKING007: u r joking.

JUNGLECAT: no I am not. I am really hot.

LIONKING007: I cant do that to u. u r very special to me.

JUNGLECAT: I was just testing u. I am proud of u dear friend. let us shake hands and promise to remain true friends for life.

LIONKING007: I promise.

JUNGLECAT:

LIONKING007: ur hand is very soft. I am feeling the heat by just holding ur hand.

JUNGLECAT: u r a compulsive flirt.

LIONKING007: I am not flirting. ur hand is really very beautiful. always keep it in ur trouser pocket otherwise it may get dirty.

JUNGLECAT: u flirt. u r teasing me now.

LIONKING007: but that was very extraordinary.

JUNGLECAT: I am extraordinary. better u also be in that class bcz ordinary people r not in my list of friends.

LIONKING007: now tell me where do u live?

JUNGLECAT: I live in a small cave in the jungles of CHANDIGARH.

LIONKING007: wow.

JUNGLECAT: happy now. have u ever come to Chandigarh?

LIONKING007: yes once when I was in school. we came here on an excursion for a day. The city is really beautiful.

JUNGLECAT: yes it is. well planned, wide roads, lot of trees, big gardens and parks and above all very little pollution. and a big shopping plaza in the centre of the city where we females can empty your pockets.

LIONKING007: r u also very fond of shopping like all other girls?

JUNGLECAT: dont worry I wont burn a hole in ur pocket. lol.

LIONKING007: lol. now u r hinting at something.

JUNGLECAT: u r stupid. I am not indicating anything, just flirting.

LIONKING007: so u r also a flirt.

JUNGLECAT: yes. extraordinary. lol.

LIONKING007: ashu, tomorrow the whole family is going to Allahabad for a cousin's wedding.

JUNGLECAT: oh. cousin?

LIONKING007: yes. maternal uncle's son.

JUNGLECAT: when will u come back?

LIONKING007: Sunday evening. will miss u.

JUNGLECAT: me too. enjoy yourself.

LIONKING007: i will try to contact u from there.

JUNGLECAT: dont bother. Just enjoy. bon voyage.

LIONKING007: thx. c u soon. take care.

JUNGLECAT: u take care.

LIONKING007: puchchhhhhhhhhh.

JUNGLECAT:

30 December 2001

It had been raining for the last three days, but Sunday morning was bright and sunny as if to welcome back my friend LIONKING. It was already nine o'clock when I got up from the bed. After refreshing myself, I had a heavy breakfast of omelette and potato-stuffed parathas.

LIONKING was returning from Allahabad by evening train, so there was nothing to do to pass time. So I decided to take Sonali to the movie.

I logged in to YM at 9 p.m. I thought LIONKING must have reached home and refreshed by now. It was very cold because of the rain during the last three days and snowfall at nearby hill station of Shimla. So I switched on the room heater and made myself comfortable on the desk chair in front of the PC. I ignored the usual storm of messages as I was looking for LIONKING. But I was really disappointed not to find him there in the lobby. Maybe his train got delayed, or maybe there had been a change in his program.

Just to kill time I scanned the list of those present in the lobby. Ruby was there. Instinctively I sent an SMS to her.

JUNGLECAT: hi Ruby

RUBY_4_U: hi dear. how r u? so nice of u to have sent me an SMS. I myself wanted to meet u.

JUNGLECAT: why?

RUBY_4_U: I just wanted to say thanks.

JUNGLECAT: what 4?

RUBY_4_U: 4 guiding me and giving me the right advice? that has helped a lot. I have changed my ways.

JUNGLECAT: good 4 u. if u need any help u r always welcome. by the way have u seen Lionking today?

RUBY_4_U: no. he no longer chats with me.

JUNGLECAT: ok. bye.

I started searching the Internet for some good jokes. After about thirty minutes, I got an SMS from LIONKING.

LIONKING007: Hi darling. how r u?

JUNGLECAT: I am fine. how was the marriage?

LIONKING007: it was real fun. there was a lot of dhol dhamaka [drum beats and noise] and dancing.

LIONKING007: Ist day it was cocktails.

JUNGLECAT: what did u wear to the party?

LIONKING007: I wore semi formals—trousers, high neck sweater and a jacket over that. u know I was looking very dashing, ready to kill.

JUNGLECAT: really? did any gal told u that or u r just imagining. self praise is no recommendation.

LIONKING007: I was the hero of the evening. every gal present there was looking only in one direction.

JUNGLECAT: your direction?

LIONKING007: no in the direction of the couple who were sitting on the stage. lol

JUNGLECAT: lol.

LIONKING007: everybody was having a gala time. drinks were freely served and dancing continued till 1.00 AM.

JUNGLECAT: did u also take drinks?

LIONKING007: yes two drinks. everybody was in high spirits. then there were dance performances by family members & friends. I also gave a solo performance.

JUNGLECAT: what song did u dance to?

LIONKING007: bachna aye haseeno, lo mein aa gaya [beware, beautiful ladies, I am here].

LIONKING007: next day it was the wedding. The usual traditional affair.

JUNGLECAT: did u miss me?

LIONKING007: yes a lot. what did u do in my absence?

JUNGLECAT: missed u and missed u.

LIONKING007: what else?

JUNGLECAT: well it has been raining during these 2–3 days. it was very chilly. Today I went to a movie with Sonali and a friend of hers.

LIONKING007: which one?

JUNGLECAT: there was no new release worth watching so we saw The Lord of the Rings.

LIONKING007: is it good?

JUNGLECAT: yes it is worth watching. it takes u into the world of fantasy and adventure.

LIONKING007: what about tomorrow?

JUNGLECAT: tomorrow is 31st Dec and time to welcome the new year.

LIONKING007: how r u going to celebrate?

JUNGLECAT: u know one of my cousins, Rohit, is organizing a party in hotel Caesers for 50 people and we have booked 16 tickets, 10 for me and my friends and 6 for Sonali and her friends. so I suppose we shall have great time. what r your plans.

LIONKING007: we r going to Gymkhana club with Mom and Dad. generally it is very crowded there. but Papa was telling that this year they r not allowing any outsiders.

LIONKING007: r we meeting tomorrow?

JUNGLECAT: ok. 11.00 AM. now it is time to get into bed.

LIONKING007: u r welcome. come on.

JUNGLECAT: maroongi [I will beat you].

LIONKING007: c u. bye.

JUNGLECAT: c u. bye.

31 December 2001

It was the last day of the year 2001. I was enjoying the heat of the morning sun, thinking about the year that had passed. There was nothing very spectacular as far as my achievements during the year were concerned. It was an eventless year except for my recent meeting with LIONKING. I was not sure how long the friendship would last. For the time, I was enjoying it.

At 11 a.m. I logged in to YM and started waiting for LIONKING. As usual there were many messages coming my way, and I chatted with a gay man for some time.

I had almost forgotten about him when I received an SMS from LIONKING. It was already 1 p.m.

LIONKING007: hi sweet heart. sorry I am late.

JUNGLECAT: np. u know just now I met a gay person.

LIONKING007: here u will find every type and kind.

JUNGLECAT: do u have any experience with the same sex, I mean in real life?

LIONKING007: no.

JUNGLECAT: I don't understand how they develop liking for the same sex. Is homosexuality genetic or acquired behavior?. I will search the net to find the answer.

JUNGLECAT: u r very late. mom is calling 4 lunch.

LIONKING007: c u in the evening. 5.00 pm will be ok.

JUNGLECAT: I am not sure. I am going with my cousin to oversea the party arrangements.

LIONKING007: ok then 7.00 pm

JUNGLECAT: that will not be possible as we girls take a lot of time to get ready for parties.

LIONKING007: yeah. I have always heard Papa complaining to my Mom.

JUNGLECAT: same here. my Mom also takes a lot of time to get ready & we are always late to the parties and functions.

LIONKING007: then c u in the morning. 10.00 am.

JUNGLECAT: again it may not be possible as it will be very late tonight. so let us keep it for 12.00 o'clock.

LIONKING007: ok. as u wish. Happy New Year in advance.

JUNGLECAT: thx. same to u. bye.

LIONKING007: bye. luv u.

JUNGLECAT: u never forget to say that.

LIONKING007: bcz I really luv u. now don't be furious.

JUNGLECAT: not today. I dont want to end the year on a sour note. so I will

also say luv u.

LIONKING007:

7

THE NEW YEAR

1 January 2002

It was past 2 a.m. when we returned from the New Year party. I was dead tired because of dancing, and moreover, I had two shots of tequila, so I was feeling very sleepy. I took off some of the clothes and fell on the bed and pulled on the blanket. Immediately I was in sound sleep.

The lights were blinking, loud music was playing, suddenly there was darkness all around, and I could hear chanting of 'Happy New Year'. Startled I opened my eyes. I was in my bed, but I could still hear 'Happy New Year'. Then it dawned on me that it was morning, and it was Sonali wishing Mom and Papa. I looked at the clock; it was 9.30 a.m. I immediately got up and went downstairs and wished Mom and Papa a happy New Year. Sonali had also come down, and we all sat there in the living room. The servant brought morning tea for all, and we exchanged notes about last night's parties.

'Let us make some resolutions for the new year,' Sonali suggested.

'Let us start with the eldest. Papa first,' I proposed.

'Your papa should go for morning walk daily at 6 a.m.,' Mom said.

'Not daily but four times a week, and not at 6 a.m. but 7 a.m.,' Papa gave counterproposal.

And it was OK'd by all.

'Your mom should also accompany me,' Papa suggested.

'No, I can't go in the morning as I have to prepare breakfast for you, Ashu, and Sonali, and I have to look after the dusting, cleaning, and washing of clothes. I will go in the evening.' Mom agreed for the evening walk, and it was OK'd.

'What about you, Ashu?' Papa asked.

'Me? Let me think,' I tried to get out.

'Ashu will take me to the movies once a week,' Sonali demanded.

'That is no resolution,' Papa interfered.

'Why not? That is done. No more arguments,' Sonali asserted.

Nobody dared to contradict her, and hence, it was agreed. Now was Sonali's turn.

'She will not ask me to go to the movies every week.'

I laughed, and Sonali made a face at me.

'She will stop throwing tantrums at every opportunity,' I teased her.

'She will try to control her temper,' Mom said. Papa was silent, but he seemed to agree.

'I will try earnestly, but I don't promise any results,' Sonali agreed reluctantly.

When everybody had made a resolution, Papa said, 'New Year's resolutions are made to be broken.'

Everybody laughed.

Suddenly Sonali got up, and putting her arms around Papa, she asked, 'Papa, when are we going to Shimla?'

'Tomorrow morning, dear,' replied Papa.

She kissed Papa and thanked him. I had almost forgotten about the Shimla trip. I was also very excited. Then we discussed what clothes, shoes, etc. we should pack and for how many days. Mom asked about breakfast, but since it was already late and she must be tired from last night's party, it was decided that we would take brunch of aloo puri from Gautam Sweets.

After brunch, I excused myself and went to my room to refresh myself. It was already 11.30, and I had a date with LIONKING at twelve o'clock.

I logged in to YM, but LIONKING was not there but joined fifteen minutes later.

LIONKING007: hi. HAPPY NEW YEAR.

JUNGLECAT: hi. same to u. may the new year bring u and ur family all the happiness, peace and prosperity.

LIONKING007: thx. I reciprocate the greetings.

JUNGLECAT: why r u late?

LIONKING007: yesterday we came back very late and hence everybody got up very late. Mom was not in a mood to cook, so me and Rajan went on my Hero Honda CBZ and brought Channa Bhatura [chickpeas curry and soft and fluffy deep-fried Indian bread] from the market and everybody had brunch.

JUNGLECAT: what a coincidence. we also had brunch with Aaloo Poori brought from the market. how was the new year party?

LIONKING007: nothing much in that. there were lot many people in the club; more than expected. There was DJ and live singers. me & Rajan danced a bit. but most of the time we were sitting on our table watching the live performances. what about u?

JUNGLECAT: we had a really enjoyable party. there were no strangers. my classmates were there. Sonali's friends were there. then my cousins and cousins' friends. we danced and danced. I took 2 tequilas and was quite high. we came back at 2.00 am.

LIONKING007: I wish I were there.

JUNGLECAT: maybe next year we shall celebrate the new year together.

LIONKING007: really?

JUNGLECAT: I hope so. by the way what is ur new year resolution?

LIONKING007: I never make any resolution which is to be broken.

JUNGLECAT: hey. come on.

LIONKING007: then lie down.

JUNGLECAT: r u sure?

LIONKING007: sure of what?

JUNGLECAT: that u will be able to do it with me.

LIONKING007: I was just joking. u r very special. even if u invite me I will not do it 2 u.

JUNGLECAT: never?

LIONKING007: not now. not at this stage of our relationship.

JUNGLECAT: thx. ur resolution?

LIONKING007: u ist.

JUNGLECAT: I will be ur true friend 4 ever.

LIONKING007: I will luv u 4 ever.

JUNGLECAT: r u serious? KK pl tell me do u really luv me?

LIONKING007: yes.

JUNGLECAT: as a girl friend?

LIONKING007: yes. u r sooooooooo sweet.

JUNGLECAT: but KK we have not met and I don't believe in this luv thing. 4 me friendship is everything. let us ist cement our friendship, then we shall see whether it develops into luv or not.

LIONKING007: ok as u say. I luv u as a friend.

JUNGLECAT: so now make some other resolution. u will never be late 4 a date with me.

LIONKING007: i agree.

JUNGLECAT: KK we have been so busy in fun chatting that we have not asked each other a very important question.

LIONKING007: what?

JUNGLECAT: how did u fare in the exams?

LIONKING007: oh my God. I did fine. I am expecting two As, one B+ and one B. what about u?

JUNGLECAT: all the four As.

LIONKING007: u r brilliant. when is the next semester starting?

JUNGLECAT: 8th Jan. yours?

LIONKING007: tomorrow.

JUNGLECAT: tomorrow I am going to Shimla.

LIONKING007: alone?

JUNGLECAT: no, with family.

LIONKING007: 4 how many days?

JUNGLECAT: 3–4 days. it depends on snowfall. If it snows we may stay longer, otherwise we shall be back after 2 days.

LIONKING007: so we shall not be able to chat for 3–4 days.

JUNGLECAT: I will try from a cyber café. but u cant wait whole day 4 me to be online.

LIONKING007: I will wait 4 u at 5.00 pm for 15 minutes every day. besides I shall also be busy in the college.

JUNGLECAT: ok. bye 4 now. c u at night.

LIONKING007: why not evening?

JUNGLECAT: me and Sonali r going 4 some shopping 4 the trip. so let us keep it for 9.00 pm.

LIONKING007: ok. bye. luv u.

JUNGLECAT: bye. c u.

9 p.m.

I had packed my bag for the Shimla trip. After dinner, I had a little chat with LIONKING.

LIONKING007: hi. what did u purchase?

JUNGLECAT: nothing much. woolen socks and a few other necessities.

LIONKING007: wish u best of journey. enjoy yourself. I will wait 4 ur return.

JUNGLECAT: thx.

LIONKING007: I have to attend college tomorrow.

JUNGLECAT: I have to leave for Shimla tomorrow morning. so let us call it a day.

LIONKING007: ok. will miss u.

JUNGLECAT: I too will miss u.

LIONKING007: luv u. bye. sweet dreams and bon voyage.

JUNGLECAT: thx. good night. cu.

8

ONE-SIDED LOVE

5 January 2002

We returned from Shimla in the afternoon at about four o'clock. The excursion was perfect, so everybody, despite the tiresome journey through the hilly terrain, seemed fresh and relaxed. We settled in the family room, and Mom asked Raju to make tea for everybody. Hot tea is always welcome when you are tired especially in winters. After taking tea, I excused myself and went to my room and had a hot shower and changed into warm casuals. LIONKING must be very annoyed as I was not able to chat with him from Shimla. I logged in to YM and opened the message box. There were three messages from LIONKING, one for each day of my absence, all saying 'Waited for you'.

It was 5 p.m., and there he was.

LIONKING007: hello cattie, u there.

JUNGLECAT: hello king. how r u ?

LIONKING007: happy to hear from u. 😊 I have been trying to get in touch 4 the last three days.

JUNGLECAT: I saw ur messages. sorry i could not get away.

LIONKING007: sazaa milegi [you will be punished].

JUNGLECAT: ready boss. Just tell me.

LIONKING007: kaan pakdo [hold your ears].

JUNGLECAT: mine or yours?

LIONKING007: yours stupid and then smile and send me a kiss.

JUNGLECAT:

LIONKING007: . how was your trip?

JUNGLECAT: perfect except for two incidents.

JUNGLECAT: first, we were walking towards the Ridge and had reached Scandal Point, suddenly a big monkey came from the left side and scared us. As we were shooing him away, another one came from the right side and snatched the bag from Sonali and leapt away. we were very scared. these monkeys at Shimla r very clever and organized.

LIONKING007: lol. what is Scandal Point?

JUNGLECAT: the Scandal Point is where the Ridge road and Mall road intersect. the story goes that the King of Patiala was smitten by the daughter of the Viceroy of India. one day while she was taking a leisurely walk at this place, he kidnapped her. from then onwards the place came to be known as the Scandal Point of Shimla.

LIONKING007: that is interesting.

JUNGLECAT: on the 3rd of Jan. we went to Naldehra and Kufri.

JUNGLECAT: Kufri was once a very well maintained place. But now it is stinking with horse dung and hill slopes are strewn with plastic bags and all sorts of other materials the tourists throw away. the authorities are not taking care to preserve this picturesque tourist place.

LIONKING007: and the 2nd incident?

JUNGLECAT: it snowed during the night and was still continuing on the 4th morning. We went out and started playing in the snow.

JUNGLECAT: there was a group of 5–6 guys who were playing among themselves. we did not pay any attention to them and continued our game.

JUNGLECAT: suddenly a snow ball hit Sonali on the side of her face and she started abusing the boys. she caught hold of one of them and was about to slap him when I interfered and dragged her away.

LIONKING007: Sonali has guts yaar.

LIONKING007: have u brought a gift 4 me?

JUNGLECAT: yes, a monkey cap. u will look very cute with it.

LIONKING007: .

LIONKING007: thx. I shall luv it.

JUNGLECAT: I will unpack the bag now and then relax.

LIONKING007: ok. take rest. dont forget to send me a few photographs.

JUNGLECAT: I will but not those which have me or my family in the frame.

LIONKING007: u still dont trust me?

JUNGLECAT: I do but in some matters u have to be discreet and move very cautiously. pl dont mind.

LIONKING007: what r u doing tomorrow morning?

JUNGLECAT: I dont know. I am still left with 2 holidays. maybe I shall sort out the photographs and order prints of a few selected ones.

LIONKING007: when r we meeting tomorrow?

JUNGLECAT: after u come back from the college.

LIONKING007: stupid tomorrow is Sunday and I don't go to college on Sundays.

JUNGLECAT: then c u at 10.30 am.

LIONKING007: ok. bye. luv u.

JUNGLECAT: bye. good night.

Sunday, 6 January 2002

I was again late for my appointment with LIONKING. He must be furious, and I was thinking of ways to appease him.

I logged in to YM, and immediately he was at my throat.

JUNGLECAT: good morning His majesty. How r u?

LIONKING007: 😖 very bad.

JUNGLECAT: very sorry. actually

LIONKING007: no excuse. If u want to save urself send me a sweet sweet kiss.

JUNGLECAT: 😗 . not one I am giving u 3.

LIONKING007: 🙂 . where were u?

JUNGLECAT: actually Mom took me with her to purchase fruits and vegetables.

LIONKING007: ok. what did u buy?

JUNGLECAT: in fruits we took apples, oranges, papaya and bananas.

LIONKING007: u take bananas?

JUNGLECAT: no stupid I eat them.

LIONKING007: lol.

JUNGLECAT: here is a joke on that. a banana seller used to sit in front of a girls hostel. three friends would buy 3 bananas daily. one day the fruit seller asked them to buy more as the bananas were of best quality. but the girls took only 3. The fruit seller said "babies sometimes u must buy bananas for eating also".

LIONKING007: lol. u r very naughty.

JUNGLECAT: no. I was not one of them.

LIONKING007: and what vegetables did u buy?

JUNGLECAT: onions, potatoes, tomatoes, green peas, carrots, cauliflower, bitter gourd, mushrooms and cucumbers.

LIONKING007: u eat cucumbers?

JUNGLECAT: no idiot. i take them.

LIONKING007: really? why cucumber, we guys are always more than ready to oblige?

JUNGLECAT: a cucumber is better than a man. want to know why?

LIONKING007: why?

JUNGLECAT: there r 101 reasons but I will tell u only a few.

JUNGLECAT: a cucumber cant make u pregnant.

JUNGLECAT: u can share it with friends.

JUNGLECAT: u can carry it in your purse.

JUNGLECAT: u can have more than one cucumber without feeling guilty.

LIONKING007: lol. more?

JUNGLECAT: a cucumber stays hard 4 a week.

LIONKING007: lol.

JUNGLECAT: a cucumber never asks "Am I the first?"

JUNGLECAT: a cucumber is not bothered whether u r a virgin or not. want more?

LIONKING007: u r really junglee [wild].

JUNGLECAT: a cucumber will always respect u in the morning.

LIONKING007: what does the last one mean?

JUNGLECAT: most men after having satisfied themselves, don't care a damn about the lady. here is a joke on that.

LIONKING007: no not now. I cant laugh any more.

JUNGLECAT: a husband and wife decided to have sex in the living room. husband was ready and waiting for the wife who had gone to change into some sexy dress. the husband was very excited to see her in a black negligee.

JUNGLECAT: suddenly her foot was caught in the carpet and she stumbled. Immediately the husband got up and took her in his arms saying "I hope u r not hurt darling. first thing in the morning I will change this bloody carpet". after having furious sex, he was relaxing on the sofa. the wife got up and went to the bathroom to clean up. on her way she again stumbled over the edge of the same carpet. the husband yelled "don't u have eyes? cant u walk carefully u bloody. u might have damaged this unique carpet".

LIONKING007: u r really wonderful. always ready 4 the occasion.

JUNGLECAT: u must possess sense of humor to enjoy these jokes. Internet is full of such jokes.

LIONKING007: u r in a different mood today. I think Shimla has done something to u.

JUNGLECAT: I was just cheering u up.

LIONKING007: thx. I am feeling very hot.

JUNGLECAT: then go cool yourself.

LIONKING007: u remember my friend Neelu?

JUNGLECAT: yes. the one whom u silently love.

LIONKING007: yesterday I talked to her about u and our friendship.

JUNGLECAT: u should not have done that. girls are very jealous and suspicious.

LIONKING007: u r right. she was very suspicious and asked me to break the relationship with u.

JUNGLECAT: really. that is ridiculous.

LIONKING007: she even asked to choose between u and her.

JUNGLECAT: that is height of insecurity.

LIONKING007: and I chose u.

JUNGLECAT: what do u mean?

LIONKING007: it is all over between Neelu and me.

JUNGLECAT: u should not have done that.

LIONKING007: she left me no choice. u r perfect for me.

JUNGLECAT: look KK, I am just a shadow, an imagination. u have made an image of me but in reality I may be a totally different person. so forget this luv thing. we r just friends and will remain so for ever.

LIONKING007: I want to meet u.

JUNGLECAT: u know it is not possible at this stage.

LIONKING007: but

JUNGLECAT: no ifs and buts. it is going to be this way otherwise we stop here before it is too late to turn back.

LIONKING007: ok as u say. u have not sent me Shimla photographs.

JUNGLECAT: I just did not get time to download these to my PC. I will do it tomorrow and by evening u will receive them before we meet.

LIONKING007: so we r meeting tomorrow evening at 5 o'clock.

JUNGLECAT: yes. give me ur e-mail id.

LIONKING007: lionking007@yahoo.com. what will u do in the morning?

JUNGLECAT: nothing particular. just relax as it is the last holiday.

LIONKING007: I have to get up early for the college, so let us bid good night.

JUNGLECAT: good night. sweet dreams. bye.

LIONKING007: bye. luv u.

7 January 2002

I downloaded the Shimla pictures from my digital camera to my PC and selected those which showed Shimla's scenic beauty with and without snowfall. From among these, I selected four best photographs and mailed them to LIONKING.

Whatever happened yesterday with KK should not have happened. I asked myself, 'Am I in any way responsible for this break-up? Was he ditching that girl for me?' He had said no, but indications were still there and that disturbed me. I decided to clarify this with KK.

I just relaxed and rested during the day. Next day, the classes for the next semester were starting. I rang up two three friends to discuss the next day's schedule. I packed my college bag and put it aside on the table. Now I was ready for another session with LIONKING.

Today I was on time and immediately got an SMS from him.

LIONKING007: hi sweet heart. how r u?

JUNGLECAT: fine. how was ur college?

LIONKING007: same as usual.

JUNGLECAT: KK tell me honestly, u r not ditching Neelu bcz u luv me.

LIONKING007: no not at all. I am not a small child. I understand that our relationship is just friendship. we have not met each other, we have not talked to each other face to face. chatting and meeting on net is just an illusion. dont worry u r not in any way responsible 4 this breakup.

JUNGLECAT: thx KK. i am very much relieved. r u tense?

LIONKING007: no not at all. even then if u want to cheer me up, send me a sweet kiss.

JUNGLECAT: puchhhhhhh.

LIONKING007: puchhhhhhh.

JUNGLECAT: let us play a game.

LIONKING007: no I cant play games with u.

JUNGLECAT: idiot. I am talking of a real game.

LIONKING007: u mean role playing game.

JUNGLECAT: stupid I will ask u a question and then it will be ur turn to ask me.

LIONKING007: pl keep my questions simple. I am not as intelligent as u.

JUNGLECAT: if ur house is on fire and u can save only one thing, what will u save? ur parents, spouse & children can take care of themselves. no choices bcz it has countless answers.

LIONKING007: perhaps my degrees and certificates.

JUNGLECAT: I will save myself. certificates can be duplicated but there cant be an other JUNGLECAT.

LIONKING007: u r right. which is the most valued possession of a person? no choices answers can be varied.

JUNGLECAT: u r right answers can be many. some possessions have material value. some have sentimental value. some r pride possessions. But according to me it is one's character, honesty, sincerity and one's integrity.

LIONKING007: great.

JUNGLECAT: if u r put in solitary confinement what is the one thing u will like to take with u?

Your favorite book/Bhagwat Geeta/Note pad &Pen

LIONKING007: Bhagwat Geeta

JUNGLECAT: why?

LIONKING007: I can read it again & again. it is the philosophy of life. ur choice?

JUNGLECAT: a note pad and pen. u cant read the same book time & again. with a note pad and pen u can write something creative.

LIONKING007: when Lionking roars? no choices.

JUNGLECAT: weak hearted wet their pants.

LIONKING007: lol. more?

JUNGLECAT: Junglecat hides in her cave.

LIONKING007: lol. more?

JUNGLECAT: junglecat sends a kiss to pacify him.

LIONKING007: . more?

JUNGLECAT: MGM movie starts. now u tell?

LIONKING007: it is to remind other animals that I am still the king of the jungle.

JUNGLECAT: lol.

LIONKING007: can u weep inside water?

JUNGLECAT: never tried. can u?

LIONKING007: don't know.

JUNGLECAT: do fish feel thirsty?

LIONKING007: why r u asking me. ask the fish.

JUNGLECAT: I love u?

LIONKING007: really. . me too from the core of my heart.

JUNGLECAT: stupid tell me whether it is a question or an answer.

LIONKING007: both bcz when u say to someone "I luv u", u r simultaneously asking him "do u also love me".

JUNGLECAT: that means when u say "luv u", u r seeking my response.

LIONKING007: yes.

JUNGLECAT: then my answer is no. we r just good friends.

LIONKING007: one day u will have to say yes.

JUNGLECAT: we will see.

JUNGLECAT: it is dinner time. Mom is calling.

LIONKING007: I have an assignment to do, so we will not meet tonight. cu tomorrow evening.

JUNGLECAT: tomorrow is my ist day at college after winter break. so I may be late. we better keep it for 9.00 pm.

LIONKING007:ok. bye. luv u.

JUNGLECAT: bye. cu.

8 January 2002

That was the first day of new semester at the college. Some of the mates were meeting after fifteen days. Everybody was in perfect mood. There was not much teaching activity in the classrooms, only briefing about subjects for the present semester, so everybody was quite relaxed. We spent a good part of the day sitting in the students centre, sipping coffee, eating dosas (a South Indian dish), and discussing about the good time we had during the holidays. I returned home late in the evening at around six o'clock. Mom served me some snacks as usual and was very pleased to learn that I had got good grades.

My date with LIONKING was at 9 p.m., so I changed clothes and left for the gym. When I came back, Papa had also come from the office, so we had dinner together. He was also very pleased to learn about my grades, and as was usual, he only patted my back and said, 'Keep it up', and that was the best encouragement for me.

At nine o'clock, I logged in to YM. LIONKING was waiting only to inform me that he was busy in doing some assignment and requested me to meet next day at 6.30 p.m.

9 January 2002

It was 6.30 p.m. and time for meeting with LIONKING.

LIONKING007: hi. very sorry 4 yesterday.

JUNGLECAT: u know saying sorry wont do.

LIONKING007: Puchhhhhhhhhh.

JUNGLECAT: Puchhhhhhh.

LIONKING007: have u got ur grades?

JUNGLECAT: yes. all 4 A grades.

LIONKING007: congrats. I am proud of u.

JUNGLECAT: what about u?

LIONKING007: 3 A and one B grade.

JUNGLECAT: great. congrats.

LIONKING007: so now we shall be a bit busier and get less time to chat.

JUNGLECAT: we will manage. what r yr future plans?

LIONKING007: there is lot of time left to think about that. what about u?

JUNGLECAT: I may go abroad 4 higher studies.

LIONKING007: I am not sure. If I get good placement I may join a job.

JUNGLECAT: when do u plan to marry?

LIONKING007: when u say yes. I will come on a horse back with a Sehra on my forehead and a sword in my hand.

JUNGLECAT: u will remain a bachelor all ur life as I am not going to say yes.

LIONKING007: no, I will not remain a bachelor as I intend to do masters. u will say yes one day. Luv can melt even stones.

JUNGLECAT: but I am made of diamond and it is the hardest material on earth.

LIONKING007: let the time come. the diamond will sparkle in my ring.

JUNGLECAT: let the time come. anyway what is there in marriage for the guys?

LIONKING007: I know they r the losers. marriage is like motichoor ke laddoo, jo khai boh bhi pachhtai aur jo na khai boh bhi [marriage is like Indian sweet, both repent, those who eat and those who don't].

JUNGLECAT: that is an old saying. the latest one is: Marriage is like a Dominos pizza, costs a lot, sounds tempting, but tastes like hell, but to taste u have to buy it.

LIONKING007: so marriage is like a mousetrap. those on the outside are trying to get in. those on the inside are trying to get out.

JUNGLECAT: marriage is an institution in which the boy loses his Bachelor's Degree and the girl gets her Masters.

LIONKING007: it means it is good 4 the girls.

JUNGLECAT: no it is equally bad for both.

JUNGLECAT: In the first year of marriage, the man speaks and the woman listens.

JUNGLECAT: In the second year, the woman speaks and the man listens.

JUNGLECAT: In the third year, they both speak and the neighbors listen.

LIONKING007: it should not be so bad in all cases. It should work in cases where both luv each other.

JUNGLECAT: for a marriages to be successful both sides have to make certain compromises. I mean it is give and take.

LIONKING007: yes u r right. the husband gives and the wife takes it all.

JUNGLECAT: lol. but ladies r impossible to be satisfied.

LIONKING007: lol.

LIONKING007: jokes apart. dont u think marriage is a must for everyone. this is the most sacred relationship between a man and a woman.

JUNGLECAT: that is true. without marriage the whole social fabric will be destroyed.

LIONKING007: since family is a basic but important unit of social structure, marriage is a must to start the family.

JUNGLECAT: u r very right.

LIONKING007: so now u r ready 4 tying the knot.

JUNGLECAT: one day I will have to.

LIONKING007: when should I come to meet ur Papa to ask 4 ur hand.

JUNGLECAT: forget that. mein kabhi haath nahi aane wali [I am not going to fall into your hands].

LIONKING007: I am the king. i have fought many battles. I am ready to fight this one also.

JUNGLECAT: u may have won many battles. but this is going to be a war. let the time come. we will see who wins.

LIONKING007: feeling sleepy. c u tomorrow.

JUNGLECAT: I am not sure bcz Sonali was asking to go to a movie. i will leave a message 4 u.

LIONKING007: ok. good night.

JUNGLECAT: good night.

LIONKING007: luv u.

JUNGLECAT: bye.

11 January 2002

No Hindi movie worth seeing was showing, so I tried to dissuade Sonali, but she was adamant, and we saw *Beauty and the Beast* which was rereleased after the addition of a song. I had left a message for LIONKING that I won't be online that day.

Next day, I came back from the university at 5 p.m., and after taking a cup of hot refreshing tea, I logged in to YM, but LIONKING was not there. He had left a message fixing the appointment for 9 p.m. So I decided to finish my assignments for the day, and after that, I watched TV for sometime before having dinner.

At 9 p.m., I was again online, and there he was.

LIONKING007: grrrrrrrr.

JUNGLECAT: mewww.

LIONKING007: how r u darling?

JUNGLECAT: fine and u my stupid friend?

LIONKING007: hale & hearty as usual.

JUNGLECAT: sorry 4 yesterday. came late from the movie.

LIONKING007: which one?

JUNGLECAT: Beauty and the Beast

LIONKING007: it sounds to be an adult movie.

JUNGLECAT: no no. it is Walt Disney animated film,

LIONKING007: u like such pure fiction films.

JUNGLECAT: films r 4 entertainment and such fairy tales r light and pure entertainment.

LIONKING007: u dont watch Hindi movies?

JUNGLECAT: i generally watch hindi movies but there has been no good release recently.

LIONKING007: which is ur all time favorite Hindi movie?

JUNGLECAT: Hum Aapke Hain Kaun [*Who Am I to You*], an entertaining romantic family drama. which is ur favorite movie?

LIONKING007: Jaane Bhi Do Yaaro [*Just Let It Go Friends*]. the best comedy I have ever seen. it is a dark satire on the rampant corruption in Indian politics, bureaucracy, news media and business.

JUNGLECAT: KK what is yr birthday date?

LIONKING007: 8th November, a Scorpion.

JUNGLECAT: I hope u have no intention of biting me.

LIONKING007: I don't bite dear ones but luv them. when is ur birthday?

JUNGLECAT: 14th September. A Virgo.

LIONKING007: I think Virgo and Scorpio r perfect match 4 luv & marriage.

JUNGLECAT: KK u r moving too fast. within a few days of our meeting u have reached marriage stage, what will happen in the coming weeks.

LIONKING007: I will be dreaming of children. 4–5 of them.

JUNGLECAT: by the time we actually meet, u will make us both old enough to be grandparents; unmarried Dada Dadi [grandparents].

LIONKING007: lol.

JUNGLECAT: kk stop this day dreaming pl. i have told u a number of times, we r just good friends.

LIONKING007: ist friendship, then luv and then marriage.

JUNGLECAT: idiot.

LIONKING007: madam whatever I am, I am yours.

JUNGLECAT: u will never reform.

LIONKING007: I would like to meet u and see how my darling cat looks like.

JUNGLECAT: u know presently that is not possible.

LIONKING007: ok then send me ur photograph.

LIONKING007: r u there?

JUNGLECAT: yes. I was thinking.

LIONKING007: what is ur decision?

JUNGLECAT: ist u send me ur photograph.

LIONKING007: ok. I will send it tomorrow. give me ur e-mail id.

JUNGLECAT: junglecat@yahoo.co.in.

LIONKING007: when r we meeting tomorrow?

JUNGLECAT: same as today.

LIONKING007: ok. bye. luv u.

JUNGLECAT: bye.

LIONKING was getting more and more romantic with each meeting. I would have to be careful. He was a nice guy and I regarded him a real friend, so I could not afford to break his heart. I would have to stop him from taking this relationship beyond friendship, as it could break his heart some day. But how?

9

THE COBWEB

12 January 2002

I returned from university at 4 p.m. and, after taking some snacks and tea, retired to my room. I was curious about LIONKING's photographs, so I immediately switched on my PC and logged in to Yahoo Mail. There was a mail from LIONKING with three attachments. I opened the mail and downloaded the attachments. There were three photographs of LIONKING which I suppose were taken during his cousin's wedding at Allahabad. One was a solo with a turban which is usually worn by relatives of the bride and groom, the other was of three boys with glasses of drinks in their hand, and the third one was a group photo. He was tall, medium built, and quite handsome for whom any girl will extend her hand.

Now it was my turn to send him my photographs. I had decided to send photographs of a girl who was neither beautiful nor ugly but quite ordinary looking, who was neither fair nor dark and who was neither slim nor very heavy but of medium build. I started searching the Internet for photographs of such a girl who had Indian looks. But I could not find any which matched my imaginary portrait of hers. I will have to do something soon; otherwise, LIONKING will accuse me of breaking my promise.

I closed my eyes, and suddenly the image of my cousin Sakshi flashed before me. She fitted my imaginary portrait perfectly. I searched through the family albums but did not find any photograph of hers. Moreover, I needed a digital photograph which I could download onto my PC. Now the problem was how to take her photographs with my digital camera. The only way was to invite her to our house with some genuine excuse. I decided to meet her the next day in the university and invite her to our house, telling her that Mom was missing her and wanted to see her.

My appointment with LIONKING was at 9 p.m., and there was a lot of time left. So I decided to devote it to studying. At eight thirty, Mom called for dinner. At the dinner table, Mom asked about Sakshi, and I told her I had not met her since the reopening of the college. Mom asked me to meet her the next day and bring her with me as she was missing her a lot. I was very pleased as everything was working to my plan.

At nine, I logged in to YM and looked for LIONKING. He was not there. I again opened his pictures and was scrutinizing them when I received his SMS.

LIONKING007: hi darling.

JUNGLECAT: hi handsome.

LIONKING007: have u recd my pics?

JUNGLECAT: yes. u r a debonair. very handsome.

LIONKING007: thx. so u like me?

JUNGLECAT: which gal would not like a guy like u.

LIONKING007: so u approve me?

JUNGLECAT: approve u?

LIONKING007: I approve u without seeing ur pics.

JUNGLECAT: then?

LIONKING007: when both of us approve each other, we should come closer.

JUNGLECAT: lo aa gayee [see I have come].

LIONKING007: yes I can feel ur breathing. now give me a hug.

JUNGLECAT: sure. but it is a friendly hug.

LIONKING007: u r sooooooooo sweet. thx.

JUNGLECAT: I suppose these pics were taken during ur cousin's wedding at Allahabad.

LIONKING007: yes.

JUNGLECAT: u look handsome in that turban.

LIONKING007: It means I look handsome bcz of the turban.

JUNGLECAT: no I did not mean that.

LIONKING007: madam 4 ur kind information I was born handsome. the nurse on duty proposed to me there and then in the OT.

JUNGLECAT: lol.

LIONKING007: when r u sending ur pics?

JUNGLECAT: very soon. today I will go to the beauty parlor for some finishing touches and then go to a studio to get myself clicked.

LIONKING007: u r really funny.

JUNGLECAT: people say photographs dont lie but mine will.

LIONKING007: what do u mean?

JUNGLECAT: nothing.

A stranger told a lady "That is a beautiful child you have there."

Lady:" That's nothing. You should see his photograph."

LIONKING007: lol.

JUNGLECAT: I am not beautiful but my photograph will be beautiful.

LIONKING007: there can be no gal more beautiful than u.

JUNGLECAT: u r a fool.

LIONKING007: thx.

JUNGLECAT: ok. bye.

LIONKING007: what is the program 4 tomorrow?

JUNGLECAT: tomorrow my cousin Sakshi may be coming in the evening and after that it will be LOHRI* celebrations.

LIONKING007: means no meeting tomorrow. will miss u.

JUNGLECAT: c u day after.

LIONKING007: don't forget to send the photographs. In ur absence i will console myself by talking to ur pic.

JUNGLECAT: ok. good night. HAPPY LOHRI.

LIONKING007: HAPPY LOHRI. luv u.

14 January 2002

The previous day, I had brought Sakshi with me from college, and while showing her our Shimla photographs, I took a few pictures of her. Mom was

---

* An Indian festival celebrated to thank God for good harvest. It signifies end of winter as sun moves into Capricorn. It is celebrated by dancing and singing of folklore around a bonfire.

very happy to meet her and was gossiping with her all the time. I dropped her at her home at 7 p.m. and then we lit the bonfire and the Lohri celebrations began.

At five thirty, I logged in to YM. Immediately I received his SMS.

LIONKING007: hi my beautiful sweet heart.

JUNGLECAT: hi. how r u?

LIONKING007: fine. how was Lohri?

JUNGLECAT: we had a lot of fun.

LIONKING007: we too enjoyed a lot.

JUNGLECAT: actually I do not like the way we celebrate our festivals.

LIONKING007: what do u mean?

JUNGLECAT: have u ever thought where from the wood comes which we burn in the bonfire?

LIONKING007: I have never given a thought to it.

JUNGLECAT: millions of bonfires r lighted this day across the country and for that millions of trees r cut thus leading to deforestation. I need not tell u the disastrous effects of cutting forests.

JUNGLECAT: further do u know how much carbon is released in the atmosphere by burning of the wood?

LIONKING007: but these festivals are our culture and tradition.

JUNGLECAT: I am not against celebrating the festival but with changing times we have to modify our methods of celebrations.

LIONKING007: u r right. we can light a small fire for ritual sake.

JUNGLECAT: KK not only LOHRI but our other festivals r also very polluting. next is Holi [festival of colours, ushers in spring season] in March. promise me u will celebrate it as a GREEN HOLI.

LIONKING007: I promise. I will use only natural and herbal colors.

JUNGLECAT: use only dry colors. no water wastage. u know every Holi we waste about 2.5 million gallons of water.

LIONKING007: among all the festivals celebrated in India, Deepavali** is the most polluting.

JUNGLECAT: u r right. Diwali is the most polluting. burning of oil and candles release carbon, bursting of crackers emit enormous quantity of toxic fumes and gases, which pollute the air to such an extent that sometimes it becomes difficult to breathe.

LIONKING007: but u must agree that we cant forget our traditions and culture and these festivals are a part and parcel of that culture.

JUNGLECAT: I don't deny that. but we have to exercise restraint while celebrating these festivals.

JUNGLECAT: we have responsibility towards future generations. we must save the environment—forests, water and air, so that our children will get clean air to breathe and clean and pure water to drink.

JUNGLECAT: and forests and crops get pure water rains and not acid rains.

LIONKING007: that is true. everybody should take this responsibility of saving the mother earth.

JUNGLECAT: I take it.

---

* Diwali or Deepavali is a festival of lights celebrated by lighting small clay lamps filled with oil and candles, bursting of crackers, and exchanging of sweets and gifts. There are many reasons for celebrating this festival, the foremost being triumph of good over evil. Goddess Lakshami [goddess of wealth] is worshipped this day.

LIONKING007: me too.

JUNGLECAT: let us develop a chain. I will write 5 mails on this and ask each one of those 5 persons to forward it to 5 more people with a similar request.

LIONKING007: I will do the same. by the way, have u sent me the photographs.

JUNGLECAT: I will send them right now. I will sign off now as I have a headache and slight fever.

LIONKING007: take care of urself. have u taken any medicine?

JUNGLECAT: I generally dont take medicine 4 small problems.

LIONKING007: u must rest. we r not meeting tonight. c u tomorrow hale and hearty.

JUNGLECAT: ok. bye 4 now.

LIONKING007: bye sweetheart. luv u.

19 January 2002

I had mailed the photographs to LIONKING. I deliberately did not go online for four days to give him enough time to think. I was sure after seeing my photographs he would stop all that talk of 'darling' and 'luv u' and would agree to my proposal of only friendship.

I logged in to YM at 6 p.m., but LIONKING was not there. I opened the message box; there were a number of SMS from him, some of which read:

'hi cattie. how r u? waiting 4 u?' 5.40 p.m., 15 Jan.

'hi darling. r u alright?' 9 p.m., 15 Jan.

'hi Ashu. where r u? u look beautiful in the pics.' 6 p.m., 16 Jan.

'hi. why r u not online 4 the last 2 days? r u alright?' 9.30 p.m., 16 Jan.

'why r u silent? pl reply. I like ur photographs.' 9 p.m., 17 Jan.

'r u ok? where r u? missing u.' 6.30 p.m., 18 Jan.

As I was reading the SMS, he came online.

LIONKING007: hi. what happened? where were u?

JUNGLECAT: I was down with viral infection. sore throat, chest congestion and fever.

LIONKING007: how r u feeling now?

JUNGLECAT: better but still very weak.

LIONKING007: I was worried. there was no message from u.

JUNGLECAT: I could not get up 4 three days. today I am feeling better.

LIONKING007: still running fever?

JUNGLECAT: no, today I am fine and may attend college from tomorrow.

LIONKING007: take care of ur health. college can wait for a day or two.

JUNGLECAT: i will review tomorrow morning.

LIONKING007: recd. the photographs. who is the gal in the photographs?

JUNGLECAT: it is me who else.

LIONKING007: u had told me u were slim & trim, fair & beautiful.

JUNGLECAT: look KK here in the chat rooms every girl is beautiful, fair and have a perfect figure of 36-24-36. And every boy here is tall, handsome and possesses a 9" organ.

LIONKING007: u mean u lied to me.

JUNGLECAT: not 2 u but 2 a stranger who later became a friend.

LIONKING007: did u tell me more lies?

JUNGLECAT: I don't know. in the beginning in order 2 impress I may have. did u tell everything truthfully?

LIONKING007: mostly but not everything. but these photographs cant be yours.

JUNGLECAT: why bcz these do not fit ur imagination.

LIONKING007: may be. but u still look beautiful in these pics.

JUNGLECAT: now u r being nice.

LIONKING007: no, I am telling u the truth.

JUNGLECAT: I know how I look like. I see the mirror daily a number of times.

LIONKING007: beauty lies in the eyes of the beholder and I find u very beautiful. u have a wonderful brain, a golden heart, a pious soul and a mature thought. what else defines beauty.

JUNGLECAT: looks?

LIONKING007: 4 me looks r superficial. u can lose the outer beauty within a minute but ur inner beauty is 4 ever. I like the way u look. i luv u even more.

JUNGLECAT: thx.

I thought to myself, *Now what?*

JUNGLECAT: during the last 4 days I have given a lot of thought to our relationship and come to the firm conclusion that only true friendship is possible between us and nothing beyond that.

LIONKING007: ok. but let the relation develop. dont be too apprehensive at this stage.

JUNGLECAT: ok. what did u do these 3–4 days?

LIONKING007: nothing particular. surfed the internet 4 some good jokes and devoted most of the time to studies.

JUNGLECAT: ok cheer me up.

LIONKING007: what is a bikini?

Bikini is a dress where 90% of the woman body is exposed.

but men r very decent.

they dont look at that 90%

they look only at the covered 10%.

JUNGLECAT: lol. idiot.

LIONKING007: boys r always idiots.

If a boy is in love, his parents will ask "idiot, who is the girl?"

If a girl is in love her parents will ask "who is the idiot?"

JUNGLECAT: I don't know about others but u r definitely an idiot.

LIONKING007: do u know benefits of a woman's milk?

JUNGLECAT: no tell me.

LIONKING007:

1. It is always fresh.

2. No need to boil it.

3. It is available in attractive containers.

4. One container free with the other.

5.The containers are magical. Fill up again & again.

6. No expiry date.

7. A cat can't steal it.

JUNGLECAT: lol. thx I am feeling much better now.

LIONKING007: want more.

JUNGLECAT: no. I am tired now. c u tomorrow. bye.

LIONKING007: take care and rest. luv u. bye.

10

GREEN IDEAS SOCIETY

23 January 2002

During the period from 19 to 23 January, I was rarely online. I met LIONKING only twice or thrice during this period and that too for very short periods, every time excusing myself on the pretext of physical weakness and backlog of studies. One month had passed since we first met. We had chatted for hours during this period. I had always stressed on friendship, whereas LIONKING had been taking steps forward towards making it a love affair, which I wanted to avoid at any cost. The ploy of sending photographs of an average-looking girl seemed to have failed. However, I decided to watch his behaviour for the next few days; if he did not stop his advances, I would reveal the truth to him. I knew that will break his heart and would be very painful for me also as I might lose a good friend, but it is always better to face the bitter truth sooner than later.

I went online at 9 p.m. and sent an SMS to LIONKING. Perhaps he was also online as he immediately answered.

LIONKING007: hi. how r u darling this evening?

JUNGLECAT: fine and congratulations.

LIONKING007: for what?

JUNGLECAT: today our friendship is 1 month old.

LIONKING007: but it seems we have known each other for many years. this has been the best period of my life. God bless my Junglecat.

JUNGLECAT: May God bless our friendship.

LIONKING007: what have u been doing?

JUNGLECAT: thinking and planning.

LIONKING007: what?

JUNGLECAT: I am planning to start an NGO [non-governmental organisation] for protection of environment.

LIONKING007: really?

JUNGLECAT: I have discussed everything with Papa and he has endorsed it.

LIONKING007: tell me the plans.

JUNGLECAT: I have thought about the name. it will be GREEN IDEAS SOCIETY. What is ur opinion?

LIONKING007: it is nice. or GREEN EARTH SOCIETY.

JUNGLECAT: I will keep that in mind. by the time formalities of registration etc. r completed I am thinking of doing a pilot project.

LIONKING007: what?

JUNGLECAT: collection of all waste materials like plastic bags etc. from the university campus and make it look neat and clean.

LIONKING007: that will be a good beginning. what is ur plan?

JUNGLECAT: I plan to do this on Valentine's Day on 14th Feb. we will hire 4 cycle rickshaws and form 4 teams of 3–4 students each who will accompany the rickshaws and distribute leaflets about environment protection.

JUNGLECAT: a jumbo bag will be placed on each rickshaw for collecting the waste materials. banners will be put on the rickshaws requesting all students to collect waste objects around them & put them in the disposal bags. we will give a rose to everyone who co-operates.

LIONKING007: the plan is feasible. not much expense involved.

JUNGLECAT: whatever the expenses of the pilot project these will be shared by me and 4–5 friends.

LIONKING007: and after that?

JUNGLECAT: as a follow up action, install 50 dust bins in the university campus.

LIONKING007: this will cost lot of money.

JUNGLECAT: the money will come from membership fees and voluntary donations.

JUNGLECAT: I have plans to repeat the same thing for all the sectors, PGI, Lake, Sector-17 shopping plaza, Rose Garden, Rock Garden, Railway Station and Bus Stand.

JUNGLECAT: we will seek assistance & participation from the local administration and MP Local Area Development fund.

LIONKING007: ur plans r fantastic and I am sure they will succeed. i am there to help u in any way u want. I am proud of u darling. i am falling more & more in luv with u.

JUNGLECAT: thx. but pl control ur feelings & sentiments.

LIONKING007: I cant hide anything from u. I am saying what I feel.

JUNGLECAT: I warn u this way we wont be celebrating anniversary of our friendship.

LIONKING007: let me see how u leave me. I am FEVICOL madam [Fevicol is a famous brand of synthetic adhesive].

JUNGLECAT: lol. save the FEVICOL u may need it to piece together ur broken heart one day.

LIONKING007: my heart will never be broken since u will be glued to me throughout my life.

JUNGLECAT: very sure?

LIONKING007: yes, I am proud of Fevicol.

JUNGLECAT: lol. KK let us call it a day.

LIONKING007: ok. bye. sweet dreams. luv u.

JUNGLECAT: bye. good night.

11

JUNGLECAT IN LOVE

27 January 2002

I had been very busy in the NGO work and had very little communication with LIONKING. It was a Sunday morning, and as usual, I was relaxing under the sun on the lawns of our house, but something was disturbing me badly. LIONKING was expressing his love more and more aggressively, which was making me more and more nervous. Something had to be done urgently before he went into deeper waters and drowned himself into this one-sided affair. At that stage, he might be able to face the reality, and our friendship might survive. Any more delay might cause irreparable damage both to his heart and our friendship. Moreover, I was becoming more and more nervous and had started feeling guilty for not having told him the truth in the very beginning. Better late than never.

The clock was showing the time to be 11 a.m. I had finished my daily chores and was ready to face LIONKING. I was very tense and jittery. I logged in to YM, and immediately he was upon me.

LIONKING007: hi darling. what is up today?

JUNGLECAT: nothing.

LIONKING007: busy in NGO work?

JUNGLECAT: yes. there is lot of work to be done.

LIONKING007: have u enrolled some members?

JUNGLECAT: yes, six r already enrolled.

LIONKING007: how much is the membership fee?

JUNGLECAT: Rs. 5000/-.

LIONKING007: can I also become a member?

JUNGLECAT: not at this stage. once the society is registered, u can also apply.

LIONKING007: Ashu what is the matter? u r behaving strangely 4 the last few days.

JUNGLECAT: I am very disturbed.

LIONKING007: why?

JUNGLECAT: i have lied to u.

LIONKING007: I have already excused u 4 that.

JUNGLECAT: not that.

LIONKING007: then?

JUNGLECAT: about my love affair?

LIONKING007: what about that? I know u r having an affair.

JUNGLECAT: u know it?

LIONKING007: who else will know if not me?

JUNGLECAT: i am serious.

LIONKING007: i have never doubted ur sincerity; that is why I understand ur feelings.

JUNGLECAT: no u don't.

LIONKING007: I know u luv me but u r feeling shy to admit it.

JUNGLECAT: stupid not u. I am having an affair with someone else.

LIONKING007:?????????????

JUNGLECAT: that is why I have been asking u time and again to control urself.

LIONKING007: ohhhhhhhhhhhhhh.

JUNGLECAT: I am sorry. I did not mean to hurt ur feelings.

LIONKING007: but u could have told me in the beginning.

JUNGLECAT: I have told u a number of times that we r good friends only and nothing more than that.

LIONKING007: I am an idiot.

JUNGLECAT: no. u r a very nice guy and a true friend.

LIONKING007: who is the lucky guy?

JUNGLECAT: his name in Montu and he is a class fellow.

LIONKING007: if u don't mind, pl tell me everything.

JUNGLECAT: don't behave like strangers. and don't feel hurt. u r and will always remain very special to me.

LIONKING007: no I am not hurt. of course I feel let down. anyway I will get over it. now tell me the whole story.

JUNGLECAT: it started when we were in B.Com- II year. when I joined college nobody paid any attention to me as I was a very ordinary looking overweight gal. i did not feel bad as I was used to it since my school days.

JUNGLECAT: during the ist year we met a number of times but never talked to each other. he was very tall, about 6', overweight like me, must be more than 90kg and medium complexion. privately we called him Motoo [fat guy].

JUNGLECAT: I liked him but did not know about his feelings. I caught his eye a few times during the class but nothing more than that. and one year passed and we got promoted to II year.

JUNGLECAT: at the beginning of II year, one day he met me at the college gate while I was entering the college and he said hello to me. I also said hello & smiled at him.

JUNGLECAT: there after whenever I looked in his direction I found him looking at me and sometimes he gave me a smile. one day when I entered college canteen, he was sitting there alone. on seeing me he got up and beckoned me to sit at his table.

JUNGLECAT: I thanked him and joined him. he was having Samosas [a triangular fried pastry filled with spiced potatoes, onions, peas, and cheese], 4 of them. He offered me the plate and I took one. he was very shy and was feeling very uncomfortable. we talked very little and left after having tea.

LIONKING007: saala Motoo [brother-in-law fat guy]

JUNGLECAT: thereafter we started exchanging smiles. we came really close during the college youth festival. we along with another girl & boy had put up a stall. At the end of the day we had earned Rs. 3500.00. we donated Rs. 2000 towards college welfare fund and spent the rest at dinner.

JUNGLECAT: there after we started meeting regularly in the college canteen and our relationship flourished.

JUNGLECAT: both of us were preparing for CAT [common admission test for MBA] and had joined Bulls Eye coaching institute where we went in the evening after college. Now we were spending a lot of time together.

JUNGLECAT: thus another year passed and now we were in final year of B.Com. we would regularly meet in the college and at the coaching institute. The institute was on the ist floor and on the ground floor there was a coffee house where we used to sit before and after the classes.

JUNGLECAT: 2–3 times we bunked college and went to see movies. Montu is a very nice guy and up to that time he had not even touched me.

JUNGLECAT: I really loved him but he was not expressing his love in words. time was passing and soon the exams would be over and we would be separated. I was getting desperate. something had to be done if I did not want to lose him.

JUNGLECAT: one day while we were having coffee at the coffee house, I took a tissue paper, put it to my mouth to get a print of my lips, folded it and handed it over to him. he was puzzled, he thought it to be a love letter and put it in his trouser pocket.

JUNGLECAT: next day I got it back with an imprint of his lips on mine. that was how we confessed our love 4 each other.

LIONKING007: does he also apply lipstick?

JUNGLECAT: no idiot. he used it to get the imprint.

JUNGLECAT: thereafter we started holding hands.

LIONKING007: did he ever kiss u?

JUNGLECAT: not until then. we decided to do MBA together from same college. so we started working very hard. first it was CAT examination, which both of us did well. then there were a number of other tests 4 different colleges.

JUNGLECAT: then we appeared for B.Com final exam. on the last day of our exams we went to disco with other friends. we had a really gala time. it was I who took the first step while dancing. I squeezed his hand and our eyes met. we went out. there was an adjoining room which was empty and there he kissed me and I reciprocated. I came there & then and he excused himself to the wash room.

LIONKING007: u fat guy.

JUNGLECAT: thereafter we could rarely meet. once or twice I lied at home and went to see him. now we were waiting 4 the results. soon the results of CAT were out. both of us had identical scores which were not good enough to get us admission in any of the IIM's but were enough to get us admission in the University Business School at Panjab University.

JUNGLECAT: both of us were happy that we would be together 4 the next two years. now we sit for hours in the Students Centre eating Dosas and sipping cup after cup of hot steaming coffee.

LIONKING007: do u really luv that lallu?

JUNGLECAT: yes very deeply. he is my darling. the nicest person I have ever met.

LIONKING007: more nicer than me?

JUNGLECAT: u r both nice in different capacities.

LIONKING007: what r ur plans?

JUNGLECAT: we plan to marry one day.

LIONKING007: do u think u will be happy with him?

JUNGLECAT: yes sure.

LIONKING007: have u talked to ur parents?

JUNGLECAT: not yet. there is lot of time to do that.

LIONKING007: will they approve him?

JUNGLECAT: why not? he is from a respectable Agarwal family, educated and above all I like him.

LIONKING007: so now there is no chance 4 me.

JUNGLECAT: u will always remain my friend.

LIONKING007: madam I am not one of those who give up so easily.

JUNGLECAT: what do u mean?

LIONKING007: i will take the chance and keep on trying. only brave hearted win the bride.

JUNGLECAT: ur choice. now I am free from any blame. i have told u everything in a very simple language.

LIONKING007: if I am not the winner, I will attend ur wedding with the fat guy as ur best friend.

JUNGLECAT: accepted. u must be feeling very bad. I am very much concerned.

LIONKING007: dont worry. i am ok. the fat guy has only won the battle, I will win the war. patience and persistence always wins.

JUNGLECAT: Mom is calling 4 lunch.

LIONKING007: r we meeting in the evening?

JUNGLECAT: in the evening I have meeting with friends for designing the banners for the pilot project.

LIONKING007: and the pamphlets.

JUNGLECAT: we have dropped the idea of distributing pamphlets as mostly people throw them away after reading them and that will pollute the environment.

LIONKING007: u r right. let us meet after dinner.

JUNGLECAT: ok. bye.

LIONKING007: bye. luv u.

He was incorrigible, but I felt relieved. Now the ball was in his court. After lunch, I rested for a while and then left at 5 p.m. to meet my colleagues.

10 p.m.

That day I did not want to disappoint LIONKING as he might be disturbed after the revelation about my boyfriend. So I went online exactly at 10 p.m. He was waiting.

LIONKING007: hello. how was the meeting?

JUNGLECAT: we have finalized the design of banners.

LIONKING007: very good.

JUNGLECAT: one of my school mates who is now a software engineer has agreed to design our web site free of cost.

LIONKING007: u r making good progress.

JUNGLECAT: all the responsibilities 4 the pilot project has been assigned.

LIONKING007: can I join u on that day.

JUNGLECAT: no. not yet. we cant meet yet.

LIONKING007: i am coming.

JUNGLECAT: coming without any stimulation?

LIONKING007: lol. chatting with u is enough stimulation.

JUNGLECAT: then go to the bathroom otherwise u will draw world map on your trousers.

LIONKING007: lol. tell me a joke on that.

JUNGLECAT: let me think. ok.

Once a guy and gal were on a date. It was dark and the road was deserted. so they started making love in the middle of the road. a truck was coming from the city side and the driver saw something in the middle of the road.

JUNGLECAT: he flashed the truck lights and repeatedly blew horn, but there was no effect on the couple. on coming very near the driver stopped the truck and shouted at the couple:

"r u deaf and blind? did not u see I was coming?"

The guy replied "mr. driver we knew u were coming. but she was coming and I was also coming but u were the only one who had breaks".

LIONKING007: lol.

JUNGLECAT: KK I am worried 4 u.

LIONKING007: don't worry. I am fine. i am a fighter, a warrior who wins ist and then fights.

JUNGLECAT: great attitude. keep it up. u deserve a kiss 4 that. here it is coming. puchhhhhhh.

LIONKING007: puchhhhhhhh. I did not know a kiss comes too.

JUNGLECAT: yes it makes others to come.

LIONKING007: u r right. i am coming, so I am going.

JUNGLECAT: going?

LIONKING007: to the bathroom.

JUNGLECAT: bye. take care. good night.

LIONKING007: bye sweet heart. luv u 4 ever.

I was trying to cheer him up, and he did not show any sign of dejection or disgust. That was good, and I felt very light and fell asleep immediately.

12

JUNGLECAT TRAPPED

31 January 2002

I had not been to the movies for the last ten to fifteen days. Sonali understood that I was very busy in the NGO work, so she had not insisted. Instead she promised that she would be coming to the university on Valentine's Day with her friends to help us in the project.

I had not met LIONKING for the last three days. At 9 p.m. I logged in to YM, but he was not there. I started searching the net for more information on environment NGOs, and I found some useful links. LIONKING came online at 9.35.

LIONKING007: hi darling.

JUNGLECAT: hi. how r u?

LIONKING007: I am fine. looks u r very busy these days.

JUNGLECAT: yes very busy in NGO work. And yesterday I had to attend a wedding.

LIONKING007: enjoyed at the wedding?

JUNGLECAT: the wedding was of daughter of one of Papa's business acquaintances. I did not know anyone there, neither the bride nor the groom nor their families. but Papa wanted whole family to attend, so I had to go.

LIONKING007: how was the wedding?

JUNGLECAT: there were more than 2000 guests. It was not a wedding but a festival.

LIONKING007: the parents of the couple must be very rich.

JUNGLECAT: yes and a marriage in the family is the best occasion to show-off ones riches.

LIONKING007: it seems u did not enjoy.

JUNGLECAT: I am deadly against such lavish and extravagant show of wealth. it is sheer wastage of fortune acquired through a lifetime of hard work.

LIONKING007: u r very right. u should be a social reformer.

JUNGLECAT: I will be one day. i will lead by example.

LIONKING007: so ur marriage will be a simple family affair.

JUNGLECAT: yes. i will invite only nears and dears.

LIONKING007: but what if my family wants a lavish wedding?

JUNGLECAT: u & ur family can have their will.

LIONKING007: but how when u want only a simple marriage?

JUNGLECAT: my views don't count 4 ur wedding.

LIONKING007: they do count. how can my family ignore the wishes of my would be bride.

JUNGLECAT: now stop this nonsense. u know I will marry Montu.

LIONKING007: but what if I win the war?

JUNGLECAT: then my ist condition for saying yes will be 'SIMPLE MARRIAGE'.

LIONKING007: ☺ .

JUNGLECAT: feeling sleepy. very tired.

LIONKING007: no problem dear. sleep well. Good night.

JUNGLECAT: good night. bye.

LIONKING007: luv u.

3 February 2002

I had been very busy during the last three to four days attending meeting after meeting. So many things had to be finalized. I completely ignored LIONKING not deliberately but because of compulsion. I was so busy that I could hardly complete my college assignments and was not taking enough rest. But now everything was falling in line.

There was no meeting that day, so I decided to meet LIONKING. I went online at 9 p.m., but he was not there. I waited for an hour, but he did not turn up. I opened the message box, there were a number of messages from him as usual. I just surfed the net to read some jokes and then at 10.30, I switched off the PC after leaving a message for LIONKING.

5 February 2002

I came early from college as I had a meeting with the CA regarding legal formalities for the registration of the NGO. After the meeting, I had dinner with the family and retired to my room. That day I had no assignment to do, so I decided to try LIONKING. He was there.

LIONKING007: hi darling.

JUNGLECAT: hi. how r u?

LIONKING007: fine. u busy?

JUNGLECAT: yes. over busy. sorry 4 ignoring u.

LIONKING007: it does not matter. I appreciate ur dedication.

JUNGLECAT: whatever I do, I give my 100% to it.

LIONKING007: I know u r very sincere. what is the progress?

JUNGLECAT: the pilot project is ready to be launched before schedule.

LIONKING007: any service 4 me madam?

JUNGLECAT: I need ur good wishes.

LIONKING007: Ashu pl let me come and help u in the project.

JUNGLECAT: pl try 2 understand u cant come at this stage. my attention will be divided. I wont be able to attend u.

LIONKING007: I will not interfere in ur work. I just want to meet u. further it is Valentine's Day.

JUNGLECAT: I will be Montu's Valentine.

LIONKING007: I just want to present a rose 2 u, nothing else.

JUNGLECAT: no u cant come. pl understand.

LIONKING007: I overrule u. I will come and present a rose to u on the lovers' day. u cant deny me the opportunity.

JUNGLECAT: pl don't be adamant like a child. try to understand my limitations as a girl.

LIONKING007: ok. I will come but will not show up. I will be watching u all the time but u will not see me. after completion of ur pilot project I will present u a rose. nobody will notice, especially the fat guy. now satisfied.

JUNGLECAT: I am not comfortable with ur plan.

LIONKING007: what if I agree now and then come without informing u.

JUNGLECAT: u cant do that.

LIONKING007: i can and I will. don't forget that I am at war with ur fat guy and I have every right to collect sensitive information about him.

JUNGLECAT: so u want to come 4 spying on us.

LIONKING007: not u.

JUNGLECAT: KK u r a true friend. u cant ignore my request. Pl don't try anything silly.

LIONKING007: I am an idiot and an idiot can only behave like an idiot.

JUNGLECAT: no u r not an idiot. u r a very nice person who is sensitive to others feelings. pl. I am sending u a flying kiss.

LIONKING007: accepted.

JUNGLECAT: thx.

LIONKING007: 4 what?

JUNGLECAT: 4 accepting my request not to come.

LIONKING007: I accepted ur kiss.

JUNGLECAT: I know u r just teasing me.

LIONKING007: no I am serious.

JUNGLECAT: 😟.

LIONKING007: so now u r using the ultimate weapon of ladies. these tears can even melt stones. i am nothing.

JUNGLECAT: so u agree.

LIONKING007: no. I know these r crocodile tears.

JUNGLECAT: no these r real. what will u gain by coming here?

LIONKING007: madam if u don't try, u cant gain anything. it is my right to try & u cant take it away from me. I have very heavy stakes. so it is final. I am coming.

JUNGLECAT: go to hell. come and come again as many times as u wish. I don't want to see u again. good bye.

LIONKING007: Ok. let me think

JUNGLECAT: bye.

LIONKING007: bye. luv u.

JUNGLECAT: I don't.

13

JUNGLECAT COMMITS SUICIDE

5 February 2002

I was very upset with LIONKING's behaviour. I was worried about what would happen if he actually came. He was very adamant on coming and had only promised to review his decision. If he came, it could create a number of problems for me.

Sakshi would be there as she was also a member of the NGO and was actively participating in the project. LIONKING would mistake her for JUNGLECAT as I had sent her photographs instead of mine. Sakshi knew nothing about it and about LIONKING. If he tried to contact her or tried to present a rose to her, there was every possibility that an unpleasant scene would be created, and I would lose both my cousin Sakshi's confidence and LIONKING's friendship. Sakshi would come to know what I had done and would never forgive me for that. She might even tell the family about my deception, and I was very afraid to face the consequences. What could I do? Suppose I took Sakshi into confidence, would she cooperate? I had doubts about her help in the matter, and further I would be taking the risk of exposing and downgrading myself in her eyes, which could otherwise be avoided if LIONKING behaved as he had promised.

There was further risk of somebody calling me by my nickname, Ashu, and LIONKING hearing it. That would be a disaster. I was in a fix, and there seemed to be no way out. I was repenting for having started all this, for creating

JUNGLECAT who had become a big liability for me. But now nothing could be done. I had committed a blunder and put my integrity at stake. The only way out was LIONKING. Or I would have to terminate everything, including my friendship with LIONKING.

After carefully analyzing every aspect of the situation, I came to the conclusion that the only way to stop the catastrophe was to persuade LIONKING to cancel his program of coming to Chandigarh. If he did not agree, I would have to finish everything. I went online at 9 p.m., but he was not there. I had no option but to wait for him. He came online at 9.20, and I pounced on him.

JUNGLECAT: hi Your Majesty.

LIONKING007: hi darling. how r u?

JUNGLECAT: fine and u?

LIONKING007: I am fine. is the temperature down?

JUNGLECAT: I am cool, I know u r a dear friend and u will do nothing which could jeopardize my reputation & honour.

LIONKING007: today u can ask 4 anything. yesterday night u saved my life.

JUNGLECAT: what r u talking about?

LIONKING007: yesterday night I had a strange dream. I am alone in a deserted street. suddenly some hoodlums who looked like monsters appeared from nowhere and advanced towards me.

LIONKING007: I began running but I was unable to run. With great effort I reached the dead end of the street and turned back. The monsters were very near. I entered the under construction building on my left.

LIONKING007: i started climbing the stairs and continued to do so for a long time but the stairs were not coming to an end. the monsters were still following me.

LIONKING007: i reached the roof of the building. there was no escape route from there. I was perspiring and soon the monsters were there. they were huge animal like creatures. one of them advanced towards me and I withdrew backwards.

LIONKING007: now I was at the edge of the roof. the monster picked me up and threw me down. I shrieked and shrieked. but before I could hit the ground, someone came flying, took me in his arms and safely placed me on the ground.

LIONKING007: i looked up in gratitude but was astonished to see that it were you, but you were a guy not a gal.

JUNGLECAT: u know sometimes dreams r true.

LIONKING007: I dont believe that.

JUNGLECAT: suppose I tell u that I am actually a guy.

LIONKING007: suppose I tell u I am actually a lion. grrrrrr.

JUNGLECAT: I am not joking.

LIONKING007: I am also not joking. I am really a lion. king of kings.

JUNGLECAT: kk be serious. I swear I am a guy.

LIONKING007: have u undergone a sex change operation. how does it feel with that tail in the front?

JUNGLECAT: it always felt very good.

LIONKING007: u mean u had it from the beginning.

JUNGLECAT: yes I was born with it.

LIONKING007: I don't believe u. u want to get rid of me. ist u said u were not beautiful. then u said u were having affair with that idiot fat guy and now u say u r a guy. what a joke.

JUNGLECAT: it is not a joke. It is reality. I agree I had lied to u about everything. the photographs were fake. I could not have an affair with the fat guy as I am not gay.

LIONKING007: 4 a minute suppose I accept what u say, why did u deceive a so called true friend.

JUNGLECAT: I still consider u a true friend. I have not deceived u. yes I did deceive a stranger. It is another matter that the stranger later became a dear friend.

LIONKING007: but why did u do this? why this id of JUNGLECAT.

JUNGLECAT: I had told u I was new to internet chatting. for the first few days I tried various sites with a male id but no girl was available 4 chatting.

JUNGLECAT: if by chance I found one, she would immediately leave. perhaps my chatting method was wrong. I did not know what to talk and how to chat. I think most of the girls dismissed me as a lallu.

JUNGLECAT: then I decided to learn how other guys chatted. so I took this id and started chatting as a gal.

JUNGLECAT: but the very first day I had an accident.

LIONKING007: an accident?

JUNGLECAT: yes. I bumped into Lionking. chatting with u was so interesting that after that I did not try anyone else. I developed a soft corner 4 u in my heart and thought I have found a real friend.

LIONKING007: but u could have told me this in the very beginning.

JUNGLECAT: I was afraid u will leave me immediately.

LIONKING007: but that I can do even now.

JUNGLECAT: that is ur choice. but I will always remember u as a friend whom I never saw or met but who was very close to my heart.

LIONKING007: I still cant believe it.

JUNGLECAT: u cant believe it or u don't want to believe it. somewhere in ur subconscious mind u had a thought that I was not a gal and that translated into ur dream.

LIONKING007: I don't agree with that. it is simple. either u want to get rid of me or u don't want me to come to Chandigarh.

JUNGLECAT: yes it is right. I don't want u to come to Chandigarh but I don't want to get rid of u.

LIONKING007: now I am definitely coming to Chandigarh.

JUNGLECAT: why after all this?

LIONKING007: I want to know the truth.

JUNGLECAT: I swear by u, this is the truth.

LIONKING007: who am I to u to swear by me?

JUNGLECAT: u r my friend and 4 me friendship is above any relation. If u wish I can swear by my Papa. I can swear by my Mom. I can swear by myself.

LIONKING007: I want to believe u. my mind says yes but my heart says no. I am in a dilemma. Let us call it a day. let me think. we shall meet tomorrow same time.

JUNGLECAT: ok. bye. good night.

LIONKING007: bye. I still luv u.

I sat there immobilized, unable to think. The inevitable had happened. I had no regrets. Actually I felt relieved and light-hearted. All the anxiety and fear was gone. I was a free bird now. I had performed my duties as a friend. I did not care what happened after that. But one job still remained to be performed.

With tears in my eyes, I had decided to commit suicide. JUNGLECAT had to commit suicide. There was no other way out of this complex dilemma. I deleted the JUNGLECAT ID from YM and deleted the Yahoo ID of JUNGLECAT. JUNGLECAT was buried in the jungles of Yahoo, and I had performed the last rites and prayed for her soul to rest in peace.

14

LIONKING KILLED

6 February 2002

Though sad yet I felt very relieved. LIONKING might or might not accept the reality, but I had revealed the truth. If he did not accept the reality, the onus would be on him. In such a case, that could be our last meeting; otherwise, we could still continue to be friends.

I was online at 9 p.m. and logged into YM with my original ID ASHU_THE_GREAT and found LIONKING waiting.

ASHU_THE_GREAT: hi Lionking.

LIONKING007: hi. how r u darling?

ASHU_THE_GREAT: I am fine. now stop calling me darling.

LIONKING007: where is JUNGLECAT?

ASHU_THE_GREAT: she is no more.

LIONKING007: what happened?

ASHU_THE_GREAT: she committed suicide last night.

LIONKING007: oh my God. this cant be true. u r joking?

ASHU_THE_GREAT: no more jokes. i am serious.

LIONKING007: but why?

ASHU_THE_GREAT: she could no more live a fake life based on lies.

LIONKING007: she was my darling.

ASHU_THE_GREAT: she is buried in Yahoo jungles. go pay ur last respects to the departed soul.

LIONKING007: :(. so what next?

ASHU_THE_GREAT: accept the fact that I am a guy.

LIONKING007: i cant. i have analyzed ur behavior and found it perfect for a girl. there had not been the slightest indication that u were a guy.

ASHU_THE_GREAT: now what proof u need? should I send my photographs?

LIONKING007: those could again be fake.

ASHU_THE_GREAT: do u have a web cam?

LIONKING007: no. do u have a phone near ur PC?

ASHU_THE_GREAT: we have a cordless phone. i will bring it in a minute.

LIONKING007: go fetch it.

ASHU_THE_GREAT: yes. I got it.

LIONKING007: give me the number.

ASHU_THE_GREAT: 0172-598269.

LIONKING007: i will call u on phone and type four questions in the chatting window, u have to answer those question on phone in ur own voice.

ASHU_THE_GREAT: ok.

The phone started ringing, and I picked it up and said hello. There was no reply from the other side, but immediately there was a question in the chat window.

LIONKING007: what was the day when we met 4 the first time?

I replied on phone, 'It was a Sunday.'

LIONKING007: where did I go to attend my cousin's wedding?

'Allahabad.'

LIONKING007: what is my full name?

'Krishan Kant Malhotra.'

LIONKING007: what is special about my friend Ruby?

'She does not wear panties.'

LIONKING007: all ur answers r correct. that means u r the same person with whom I have been chatting and u r speaking in a male voice, so I have to accept that u r a guy, unless u r an expert at changing the voice.

ASHU_THE_GREAT: but why r u not talking on the phone?

LIONKING007: I don't want to shock u.

ASHU_THE_GREAT: pl come on the phone.

LIONKING007: ok. 'Hello.'

Me: Who is that?

LIONKING: Radhika.

Me: Who, Radhika?

LIONKING: Radhika, The LIONKING.

Me: What do you mean? You are a girl, LIONKING is a girl.

Radhika: Yes.

Me: How can I be sure that you are the LIONKING? You may be faking your voice to take revenge on me or someone else may be speaking as Radhika.

Radhika: You can check the same way as I checked.

Me: What is the name of my sister?

Radhika: Sonali.

Me: What is the name of my cousin?

Radhika: Sakshi.

Me: What is the name of the NGO I am starting?

Radhika: Green Ideas Society.

Me: What is my full name as told to you?

Radhika: Abhilasha Gupta.

Me: You have passed the test. But why did you have to do this?

Radhika: Somewhat similar reasons. When I tried to chat with my original ID, BeautifulRadha, there was a flood of invites from the guys, but everybody was interested in sex only. I did not know how to handle these sex-hungry guys. So I decided to learn how other girls behaved in such a situation, and I took this ID of LIONKING007 and started flirting with the girls. But then I met a girl with the nickname JUNGLECAT, and I learnt what real chatting was all about. Chatting with you was so interesting that I did not want to lose you at any cost.

Me: So you have been making a fool of me.

Radhika: And you were making a fool of me.

Me: Actually we were not making a fool of each other. The fact is that we both are the biggest fools on this earth. Hahahaha.

Radhika: You are right. We are idiots. Hahahaha.

ASHU_THE_GREAT:

LIONKING007:

ASHU_THE_GREAT: now what?

LIONKING007: we continue as friends.

ASHU_THE_GREAT: let us exchange sex.

LIONKING007: what do u mean?

ASHU_THE_GREAT: now I will be Lionking and u will be Junglecat.

LIONKING007: that is a nice idea.

ASHU_THE_GREAT: with heavy heart I request u to kill Lionking, so that he can take new birth.

LIONKING007: is that necessary?

ASHU_THE_GREAT: yes. we have got used to our fake nicknames. chatting with our original names is very dull.

LIONKING007: ok. I will kill him right now. u just wait for 5 minutes.

Radhika was back soon.

BeautifulRadha: LIONKING007 is killed. I buried him alongside Junglecat in the YAHOO jungles.

ASHU_THE_GREAT: u can immediately take Junglecat id before anybody else takes it. I will take Lionking id.

BeautifulRadha: promise me u will continue to be a true friend as before.

ASHU_THE_GREAT: I promise we will remain true friends 4 ever.

BeautifulRadha: further we will not talk again about our previous lives as Junglecat and Lionking.

ASHU_THE_GREAT: agreed.

BeautifulRadha: we should not feel sorry for Junglecat and Lionking as they r taking birth again.

ASHU_THE_GREAT: u know why u r idiot.

BeautifulRadha: why?

ASHU_THE_GREAT: bcz I am stupid.

BeautifulRadha: lol. so now we r even before we start a new relationship.

PART II

1

REBIRTH

10 February 2002

That was a Sunday morning, and as usual, I was sitting on the back lawns of our house, sipping tea, and scanning the Sunday newspapers. I had not been in contact with Radhika since the day we exchanged sex. I had been very busy for the last few days as the date for pilot project of Green Ideas Society was drawing nearer. The success of the pilot project was very vital for my future plans for the NGO; hence, I was sparing no effort. Earlier I did not want LIONKING to come to Chandigarh at the launching of the pilot project as I feared my fake identity would be exposed. Since ultimately everything had to be disclosed and JUNGLECAT and LIONKING had to sacrifice their lives for the sake of truth, I was wishing for Radhika to come and stand shoulder to shoulder with me at the launching of the pilot project.

The old relationship of JUNGLECAT and LIONKING was based on lies and deception; hence, it was destined to end sooner or later. The new relationship would be based on truth and trust, hence would be more stable and durable. We had developed a bond of friendship which was expected to grow stronger with the change in roles.

I logged in to YM at 11 a.m. and entered the Flirt Chat lobby. I scanned the list of those present in the lobby. Radhika or JUNGLECAT was not there. I decided to wait as I was trying to meet her without appointment. I was not in a mood to chat with anybody else, so I just waited for her. I was reflecting on our past relationship and thinking about the type of relationship we would be maintaining in the future. Suddenly JUNGLECAT jumped upon me.

JUNGLECAT: hi Lion.

LIONKING: hi cattie. how r u?

JUNGLECAT: fine and u?

LIONKING: what is up?

JUNGLECAT: now u r taking revenge.

LIONKING: now it would be better if u dont ask me that question.

JUNGLECAT: why?

LIONKING: bcz now I have something which can be up.

JUNGLECAT: lol. what about the pilot project?

LIONKING: it is ahead of schedule. I wish u could be there.

JUNGLECAT: I also wish the same but u know it is not possible.

LIONKING: I understand. how did u handle the sex change?

JUNGLECAT: some deletions and additions were made but it was very painful, both physically as well as psychologically when they took out half of my brains.

LIONKING: why?

JUNGLECAT: to make me a perfect female.

LIONKING: u were already an idiot, what now?

JUNGLECAT: I will be maha idiot [great idiot].

LIONKING: means that if u now find a banana peeling in ur way, u will have to slip on that.

JUNGLECAT: yes. lol.

LIONKING: lol. I want to present u my old trousers which had a hole in one pocket.

JUNGLECAT: why?

LIONKING: I cant get into them anymore.

JUNGLECAT: that u wont be able to even if I wear them.

LIONKING: lol. once a painter was standing on a staircase and painting the front of a building.

LIONKING: a beggar asked him 4 alms. He came down the staircase. As his hands were soiled, he asked the beggar to take some money from his left pocket.

LIONKING: the beggar put his hand in the pocket but it had a big hole in it. the painter asked him to try the other pocket.

LIONKING: the beggar put his hand in the other pocket but it had also a big hole.

LIONKING: the beggar told the painter" sir, u r lucky to have two, but u r poorer than me."

JUNGLECAT: lol. u r very naughty.

LIONKING: lol.

JUNGLECAT: let us start everything afresh.

LIONKING: but we have not yet done anything.

JUNGLECAT: lol. pl be serious.

LIONKING: what do u mean?

JUNGLECAT: first let us know each other.

LIONKING: but we already know each other and we r friends.

JUNGLECAT: whatever we know about each other are either half truths or half lies.

LIONKING: u r right. let us be sincere & truthful and swear not to lie again.

JUNGLECAT: yes. henceforth only truth. either of us will ask a question & we both shall reply to that.

LIONKING: ok. should we start?

JUNGLECAT: yes. a/s/l.

LIONKING: 26/m/Chandigarh.

JUNGLECAT: 23/f/Delhi. Qualification?

LIONKING: I have done Masters in Chemical engineering from Panjab University and now doing MBA final year from University Business School.

JUNGLECAT: done B.Com (Hons) and now doing MBA final year from Faculty of Management Studies, Delhi University.. what is ur specialization in MBA?

LIONKING: Marketing. yours?

JUNGLECAT: Finance.

LIONKING: from which college u did ur B.Com (Hons.)

JUNGLECAT: Lady Sri Ram College, Delhi.

LIONKING: what r ur future plans?

JUNGLECAT: campus placements have already started. if I get placement in some good company, I will do job for 2–3 years and then marriage.

LIONKING: would u continue the job after marriage?

JUNGLECAT: that would depend upon so many things.

LIONKING: like?

JUNGLECAT: my ambitions, my husband's wishes, my in- laws status, family's financial conditions and children etc. etc.

LIONKING: how many kittens do u plan to produce?

JUNGLECAT: that would be decided after marriage in consultation with my husband.

LIONKING: that's like a nice gal.

JUNGLECAT: real name?

LIONKING: Ashish Gupta. nick name Ashu.

JUNGLECAT: Radhika Malhotra. nick name Radha.

LIONKING: mere man ki ganga aur tere man ki jamuna ka, bol Radha bol, sangam hoga ke nahin [tell me, Radha, if Ganges of my heart and Jamuna of yours will ever be joined].

JUNGLECAT: nahin, kabhi nahin [no, never].

LIONKING: don't be so cruel. pl say yes.

JUNGLECAT: I will think over it but 4 now we r only friends.

LIONKING: I am joking. we r real friends and shall remain so.

JUNGLECAT: family details?

LIONKING: whatever I told u earlier is the truth.

JUNGLECAT: I have also told the truth. what r u wearing?

LIONKING: blue jeans, white shirt and grey sweater.

JUNGLECAT: I am wearing a multicolor Punjabi suit and black sweater. which is ur favorite color?

LIONKING: r u planning to present me a shirt? i think white will be ok.

JUNGLECAT: stupid.

LIONKING: I am wearing my favorite colors.

JUNGLECAT: my favorite colors r—bright yellow, red, pink, light purple and maroon.

LIONKING: any left out.

JUNGLECAT: yes I like blue and green also.

LIONKING: why dont u say that u like all the colors except black and white and these r my favourite colours.

JUNGLECAT: thats interesting.

LIONKING: r u wearing nothing underneath? thats very sexy and convenient.

JUNGLECAT: did u tell what u are wearing underneath?

LIONKING: nothing.

JUNGLECAT: is that not sexy?

LIONKING: it is convenient.

JUNGLECAT: lol. I am wearing white bra and panties with floral pattern.

LIONKING: that must look very beautiful.

JUNGLECAT: what?

LIONKING: the floral pattern.

JUNGLECAT: I am not such an idiot. I understand what u meant.

LIONKING: forgive me. I know u have long nails and sharp teeth.

JUNGLECAT: lol. are u veg or non-veg?

LIONKING: lions r pure non-veg but I am a domesticated lion, so take both veg as well as non-veg. my Mom is pure veg but Papa, Sonali and me occasionally take non-veg, but we don't cook non-veg at home except for eggs.

JUNGLECAT: our family is both veg and non-veg. we cook non-veg at home also. what is ur favorite dish in veg?

LIONKING: sarson ka saag with makai ki roti served with butter, green chilli pickle and shakkar or gur [mustard green leaves cooked with spinach and served with cornbread, butter, green chilli pickle, and jaggery].

JUNGLECAT: that is also my favorite.

LIONKING: then u r invited. Mom has prepared it 4 lunch.

JUNGLECAT: thx. don't eat the whole of it alone, pl save something 4 me also.

LIONKING: what is ur favourite in Non-Veg?

JUNGLECAT: chicken butter masala and chicken briyani.

LIONKING: I like cream chicken and roasted fish.

JUNGLECAT: I dont like fish. It smells a lot.

LIONKING: can u answer a question on that?

What did fish smell like before Eve went swimming?

JUNGLECAT: i don't know as I was not born at that time.

LIONKING: What did Eve smell like before she went swimming?

JUNGLECAT: I don't know as I did not smell Eve before or after that.

LIONKING: u r a real idiot. cant u make anything out of the two questions?

JUNGLECAT: what? oh, u have a real dirty mind? Lol.

LIONKING: lol.

LIONKING: Radha it is time 4 lunch. and I want to take it leisurely. I have to ask Mom to add extra tomato to my Saag as I like it a bit sour.

JUNGLECAT: dont forget to remember me with each bite.

LIONKING: sure.

JUNGLECAT: r we meeting in the evening?

LIONKING: no. I am meeting friends in the evening. may be after dinner.

JUNGLECAT: ok. bye.

LIONKING: bye.

10 p.m.

LIONKING: hi idiot.

JUNGLECAT: hi stupid. did u enjoy the lunch?

LIONKING: yes.

JUNGLECAT: u know I was feeling jealous, so I asked Mom to cook the same 4 dinner.

LIONKING: one day we shall cook & eat the delicacy together.

JUNGLECAT: I shall be waiting 4 that day.

JUNGLECAT: do u have a girl friend?

LIONKING: girl friends r very difficult to find these days.

JUNGLECAT: what do u mean?

LIONKING: u know the sex ratio is declining every year. figures for 2001 census have been released recently. the all India sex ratio [female/male population] is 933.

JUNGLECAT: what does it mean?

LIONKING: it means there r 933 females for 1000 males.

JUNGLECAT: that means population of females is declining.

LIONKING: yes. for Delhi it is even less at 821 and for Chandigarh it is worse at 773. that means about 25% of the male population of Chandigarh will not be able to find a girl friend.

JUNGLECAT: the long term consequences can be very disastrous.

LIONKING: not can be but will be. if only 75% of the population is married, and able to produce children, a day will come when human race will be wiped out from the earth.

JUNGLECAT: for the present this imbalance can lead to social unrest.

LIONKING: yes. there will be fights among males for possession of a female. Crimes against women like rape, sexual harassment, molestation, verbal abuse, torture, exploitation and kidnappings etc will increase.

LIONKING: this will lead to increase in human trafficking and even trading in females.

JUNGLECAT: oh my God.

JUNGLECAT: but what r the reasons for this low sex ratio?

LIONKING: the basic reason for this is the age old traditions, customs and beliefs of the Indian society that give preference to a male as he is likely to continue the family lineage.

LIONKING: and he is considered the bread winner in the family. a girls leaves her parents house after marriage and it is the male child who lives with the parents and takes care of them in old age.

LIONKING: such narrow-minded people, whenever they discover they are going to have a girl child (through illegal sex selection tests), get the fetus aborted.

LIONKING: u know about half a million female fetuses are aborted every year and about 10% of the girls born in India do not see their first birthdays.

JUNGLECAT: the problem is very serious. What is the solution?

LIONKING: the first and foremost is the empowerment of the female through education.

JUNGLECAT: and the pre-natal sex determination tests should be totally banned.

LIONKING: such tests r already banned but some doctors still continue to do such tests in the guise of checking the pre-natal health of the fetus.

JUNGLECAT: the parents opting for such test and the doctor conducting such test should be arrested and charged with murder.

LIONKING: Radha why dont u do some work in this field.

JUNGLECAT: what can I do?

LIONKING: Radha u r a brave and intelligent girl. First talk to ur friends and class mates, then involve your nears and dears and from their suggestions, make a strategy and plan about what is to be done, how it is to be done and when it is to be done.

JUNGLECAT: let me think about it. i understand it will be a great service to the whole womanhood, society and my country.

LIONKING: dont worry, I will always be there for discussions and help.

JUNGLECAT: u r really a great thinker.

LIONKING: thx. there is nothing great in it. Radha I am feeling sleepy.

JUNGLECAT: ok. tomorrow?

LIONKING: not sure. just check at 10.00 pm.

JUNGLECAT: ok. bye and good night.

LIONKING: good night. sweet dreams.

2

MEETA AND ABHI

11 February 2002

At 10 p.m., I logged in to YM and found JUNGLECAT was waiting.

JUNGLECAT: good evening your majesty.

LIONKING: good evening sweet heart.

JUNGLECAT: yesterday u did not answer my question.

LIONKING: which one?

JUNGLECAT: do u have a girl friend?

LIONKING: yes, I have. her name is Meetali, nick name Meeta.

JUNGLECAT: tell me a little bit more.

LIONKING: she is a class fellow. our relationship is one year old and we have confessed to each other. I have dated her 2–3 times but we have not gone beyond holding hands.

JUNGLECAT: do u plan to marry her?

LIONKING: yes. we have decided to marry each other.

JUNGLECAT: have u told ur parents about her.

LIONKING: not yet, though she has come to my house twice and Mom has met her.

JUNGLECAT: does ur Mom like her?

LIONKING: I don't know.

JUNGLECAT: will ur parents agree 4 the marriage.

LIONKING: though it will be an inter-cast marriage but I don't see any problem. my parents r quite broad minded and they love me too much and I suppose they will readily agree for the marriage.

JUNGLECAT: what about Meeta's parents?

LIONKING: she is confident of getting their consent.

JUNGLECAT: does she belong to Chandigarh?

LIONKING: no. she belongs to Ludhiana and is staying in the university hostel.

JUNGLECAT: does she know about me?

LIONKING: yes.

JUNGLECAT: introduce me to her when u think it to be ok.

LIONKING: oh sure and I promise you that I wont marry her or any other girl without ur approval.

JUNGLECAT: thx for the trust and I promise you the same.

LIONKING: do u have a boy friend?

JUNGLECAT: Yes, I have. his name is Abhishek, nick name Abhi.

LIONKING: how old is yr relationship?

JUNGLECAT: almost two years. since we joined MBA.

LIONKING: have u confessed to each other?

JUNGLECAT: yes. classical style. one day he held my hand and said "Radha, I love u, do u?" and I just nodded in agreement with my eyes closed.

LIONKING: have u discussed marriage plans?

JUNGLECAT: yes. we plan to marry after two years.

LIONKING: have u introduced him to ur parents?

JUNGLECAT: not yet. I will do that after we complete MBA and get good jobs.

LIONKING: his job may move him outside Delhi. so do it now before he leaves Delhi.

JUNGLECAT: Ashu there is one problem or u can say it is my apprehension. He belongs to a backward class, but his family is high class. both his parents are I.A.S. officers of Haryana cadre. my parents may object bcz of his caste.

LIONKING: Radha, though we youngsters no longer believe in the caste system, the previous generation may still have reservations. so it would be better if u disclose ur affair to ur parents at the earliest.

JUNGLECAT: his parents have no objection. I have already met them and Abhi told me they have approved me.

LIONKING: good. so half the battle is won. I am confident u will be able to convince ur parents.

JUNGLECAT: very soon I will invite him to my house.

LIONKING: have u discussed our relationship with him?

JUNGLECAT: he is not positive about internet friendships, but he has no objection to our friendship.

LIONKING: can I meet him someday?

JUNGLECAT: u will have to meet him as without ur approval I am not going to marry him.

LIONKING: now one thing is decided that we r going to be true friends only nothing more than that.

JUNGLECAT: yes. u have a GF and I have a BF and we respect each others' emotions, so we promise each other to be only friends for ever.

LIONKING: agreed. Here is a quote on love:

"Lucky is the woman who is first love of a man and luckier is the man who is last love of a woman."

JUNGLECAT: what does it mean?

LIONKING: it means u r lucky to be the ist love of Abhi, as he wont have any hang up of his previous love. And I will be luckier if I am the last love of Meeta as she will remain mine forever.

JUNGLECAT: what a thought.

LIONKING: u will learn many things if u keep company of intelligent people like me.

JUNGLECAT: do u mean I am a duffer?

LIONKING: I don't have to tell u that.

A lady went to a doctor for check up. After thoroughly examining her, the doctor told her "Congratulations. You are pregnant." The lady "Is it mine?"

JUNGLECAT: I am not that stupid.

LIONKING: agreed u r not that stupid but u agree u r.

JUNGLECAT: one day u will know who is more intelligent.

LIONKING: that day is today and today I know u r an idiot.

LIONKING: and I am a great idiot. now happy.

JUNGLECAT: 🙂. Luv u.

LIONKING: with his OBC status, Abhi can easily get into Central Civil Services like his parents. why does not he try for that after completing MBA.

JUNGLECAT: he has plans to do that and I am sure he will be selected.

LIONKING: on merit or bcz of OBC [other backward class] status.

JUNGLECAT: what do u mean?

LIONKING: no offence intended, but do u think he should be eligible for availing reservation quota for OBCs.

JUNGLECAT: why not, he belongs to an OBC?

LIONKING: and his children will also be categorized as OBCs.

JUNGLECAT: yes.

LIONKING: but his family is no longer backward. neither economically nor socially. he enjoys all the facilities and even more than the so called upper castes. The social status of the family is better than most of us.

JUNGLECAT: if we take status of the family as criterion for reservation then he does not deserve preferential treatment.

LIONKING: the law needs to be changed. benefit of reservation, if it is to be given at all, should be limited to only once in the history of the family. If any ancestor or parent has already enjoyed that benefit, then it should not be available to the present generation.

LIONKING: the present system of reservation does not help in bringing the family out of the caste system but it provides incentive to the family to remain as an OBC bcz of the benefits attached with it.

JUNGLECAT: u r right. then there is no rationale in giving multi layered reservations. first reservation in education institutions, then reservations at the time of selection for a job and lastly reservation for promotion in the job.

LIONKING: this is ridiculous. I am in favor of abolishing all types of reservations. instead the SC, ST and OBCs should be provided free education, free books, free tuitions and free stay in hostels. In short all expenses for their education should be borne by the Govt.

LIONKING: make them capable not dependent.

JUNGLECAT: if more than 50% seats in educational institutions and 50% of the jobs r reserved for different categories, where will the general category students go.

LIONKING: they will go abroad as it is easier to get into a reputed foreign institution than getting into an IIM or IIT. u and I could not get into an IIM but many SC, ST or OBC students who were placed much lower than us got admission. this causes heart burns.

JUNGLECAT: and it breeds inefficiency in the system. These reserved category students get admissions into premier institutes in spite of being less intelligent than other students, then they don't work hard as they know they will be able to get a good job under reservation quota.

JUNGLECAT: even after getting the job, they don't work sincerely as they are sure of promotions before their colleagues. The system is totally unjust and it is imposed on us in the name of natural justice.

LIONKING: in ancient times one's caste was decided by ones profession but along the way the basis was changed to birth. And now the politicians r playing game of vote banks and r taking advantage of the caste system for promoting their self interests.

JUNGLECAT: how can the system be changed?

LIONKING: it is so well entrenched that nobody dares to change it. neither the SC, ST and OBCs want to move out of their caste bcz of the benefits nor any law maker or politician dares to change the system for fear of losing votes of these castes.

JUNGLECAT: why don't upper castes resist such reservations?

LIONKING: the so called upper castes have been side lined in the present political system. It is the other castes which call the shots. but a day will come when backward classes will realize that they can move upward the social ladder only if they break free from this caste system, otherwise the politicians will keep them tied to lowest step of the ladder.

JUNGLECAT: it is a vicious circle. a man is backward bcz he is backward. it is he himself who can break away from this system.

JUNGLECAT: let us hope our children wont suffer bcz of the reservations and will have equal opportunity.

LIONKING: if the system continues, a day will come when the so called upper castes will be treated as OBCs and today's OBCs will become upper castes.

JUNGLECAT: that is awful. It cant get that worse. I wont let my children suffer bcz of this disease.

LIONKING: but what if u marry Abhi?

JUNGLECAT: I will not let my children be classified as OBCs. I shall give them my name.

LIONKING: do u mean ur children will be known as Malhotras.

JUNGLECAT: yes, why not. the constitution of the country guarantees gender equality.

LIONKING: will u settle the issue before marriage or after the birth of ur ist child?

JUNGLECAT: I don't know at present but I know one thing for certain that they will not belong to any OBC.

LIONKING: three cheers. Let us call it a day on this positive note.

JUNGLECAT: good night.

LIONKING: good night.

3

SEX EXPERIENCES

13 February 2002

10.30 p.m.

I went online just to wish Radha on Valentine's Day as next day was D-day for me as the pilot project of Green Ideas Society was going to be launched, and I was likely to be very busy the whole day. The future of my plans for Green Ideas depended on the success of the pilot project. She was not online, so I left a message for her wishing her a happy Valentine's Day.

15 February 2002

10 p.m.

I had been very busy during the last two days. On Valentine's Day, I was totally occupied in the pilot project, and in the evening, we celebrated the success of the project over dinner. Suddenly I heard a buzzing sound; it was Radha.

JUNGLECAT: hi sweetie.

LIONKING: hi darling.

JUNGLECAT: tell me about the success of the Pilot Project.

LIONKING: it was a tremendous success. every student participated enthusiastically and within two hours the whole university was clean.

JUNGLECAT: very good. when r u installing the dust bins?

LIONKING: from tomorrow. yesterday we met the Vice- Chancellor and appraised him of our plans. He gave permission for installation of dust bins and greatly appreciated our initiative.

LIONKING: he also promised financial assistance after getting necessary approvals. We have enrolled him as an honorary member.

JUNGLECAT: congratulations. keep it up. how did u celebrate the Valentine's Day?

LIONKING: by cleaning the university campus and presenting a rose to Meeta and hugging & kissing her.

JUNGLECAT: that is also remarkable progress. did u kiss her on the lips?

LIONKING: on the cheek and she reciprocated.

JUNGLECAT: did it stimulate u?

LIONKING: u r a real idiot. of course it id.

JUNGLECAT: u know when Abhi once kissed me lightly on the lips, I came running.

LIONKING: came running? why?

JUNGLECAT: stupid.

LIONKING: why do u girls come at the drop of a hat?

JUNGLECAT: bcz we don't have to bother about drawing the world map on our jeans.

LIONKING:

JUNGLECAT:

LIONKING: if u don't mind tell me how far have u gone with Abhi.

JUNGLECAT: not beyond that kiss.

LIONKING: do u have any sex experience?

JUNGLECAT: no girl will ever admit to that, but since I am under oath of friendship I will tell u the truth.

LIONKING: the truth?

JUNGLECAT: and the truth is

LIONKING: yes come on.

JUNGLECAT: the truth is that I am still a virgin.

LIONKING: u r becoming very naughty.

JUNGLECAT: but I have been a victim of child abuse.

LIONKING: oh. when and how? who was the bastard?

JUNGLECAT: Papa was posted at Ahmedabad at that time. I was in 5th standard and about 10 yrs old. A distant cousin of Mom used to visit our house quite frequently.

JUNGLECAT: one day Mom and Papa had gone to see a movie and I was alone at home. Mom's cousin came and finding me alone, he started to take advantage.

JUNGLECAT: he kissed me and made me sit on his lap and compelled me to do it for him with my hand.

LIONKING: such people who exploit innocent children should be hanged.

JUNGLECAT: when Mom & Papa came back I told them that uncle had come and stayed for two hours. Mom started enquiring about his activities and I told her what had happened.

JUNGLECAT: I dont know what happened after that but I did not see that person again.

LIONKING: u know most of the cases of child abuse are by some acquaintance or by relatives.

JUNGLECAT: the incident sometimes still haunts me.

LIONKING: try to forget it as a bad dream.

JUNGLECAT: oh yes. I have more or less forgotten it.

LIONKING: I am sorry u had to recall it 4 me.

JUNGLECAT: does not matter. but now cheer me up with some interesting experiences of yours.

LIONKING: to tell u the truth I have had sex twice. first time I did it when I was in school, in 12th standard. She was a neighbor and studied in the same class but in a different school.

LIONKING: she often came to our house to take my help in studies. She was beautiful and sexy and as is the desire of every boy at that age I wanted to have sex with her.

LIONKING: one day when she came I was alone at home. I took her to my room and told her I loved her. she smiled and we kissed and had sex.

JUNGLECAT: did u enjoy it? I know that is a stupid question to ask.

LIONKING: frankly no bcz the thing was not to my expectations.

JUNGLECAT: lol. and second time?

LIONKING: I was in 2nd year of B.E. and a friend of mine lived in a rented room in Sector-15. I often visited him and had a key to his room. one day when I went to see Ramesh, he was not there. I opened the lock and lay down on his bed.

LIONKING: after about ten minutes there was a knock on the door and daughter of the land lord entered. She told me Ramesh had gone to Ludhiana. She took a chair and started gossiping. Her parents were away and she was alone at home.

LIONKING: she started cracking jokes, ist veg and then non-veg. then on the pretext of telling me my future she took my hand and squeezed it. she also leaned forward to show me her braless assets.

LIONKING: then while reading the lines of my hand she told me I was likely to have sex in the next five minutes and winked at me and we had sex twice and that time I really enjoyed it.

JUNGLECAT: did u do it again with her?

LIONKING: later I came to know she was having physical relations with my friend also. so I stopped visiting my friend and never saw her again.

JUNGLECAT: lucky guy.

LIONKING: r u jealous?

JUNGLECAT: frankly yes. I wish I was a boy.

LIONKING: lol.

JUNGLECAT: any past affair?

LIONKING: not really. only teenage crushes. when I was in school I had a crush on one of the teachers.

JUNGLECAT: result?

LIONKING: I had to work like an ass at the time of her wedding.

JUNGLECAT: lol. serves u right.

LIONKING: I did nothing wrong I just liked her and peeped into her blouse a few times. other boys also did that.

JUNGLECAT: and that was enough to make u hot.

LIONKING: yes more than sufficient. did u have any affair before Abhi?

JUNGLECAT: like u I also had a crush on one of my classmates when I was in B.Com II year. he was very handsome and I always stared at him with a strange desire.

LIONKING: what was ur desire?

JUNGLECAT: to have sex with him.

LIONKING: wow. the unlucky fellow. he must be suffering from chronic cold.

JUNGLECAT: why?

LIONKING: otherwise he could have smelled that u were ready.

JUNGLECAT: lol. every time I thought of him I got hot and had to cool myself.

LIONKING: tell me frankly did u ever had sex with him in ur imagination or dreams.

JUNGLECAT: yes. so many times.

LIONKING: luckier than me.

JUNGLECAT: how can u say that. lol.

LIONKING: lol. bye. good night.

JUNGLECAT: feeling hot. go cool yourself. good night.

4

THE BOYFRIEND

18 February 2002

According to my New Year resolution, I was supposed to take Sonali for a movie once every week. But Sonali had not proposed to see any movie for the last one month. Instead she had been helping me in the NGO work. She came to the university with her friends for the launching of the pilot project. She was taking keen interest in designing the banners and stationery, etc.

The date for the next step i.e. for PGIMER (Post Graduate Institute of Medical Education and Research) had been fixed for next Sunday, 21 February. The work was progressing as per schedule. Permission from director of PGIMER had been received. We had enrolled the director as an honorary member and two senior doctors and three junior doctors as regular members. I was very busy in organizing the things, hence was not able to meet Radha for the last two to three days.

At 10 p.m., I logged in to YM and looked for Radha. She was there but busy. I sent her an SMS, and immediately she was with me.

JUNGLECAT: hi king. How r u?

LIONKING: fine. what have u been doing?

JUNGLECAT: nothing much. waiting 4 u.

LIONKING: sorry I was busy in the NGO work.

LIONKING: how is Abhi?

JUNGLECAT: he is fine. he is always enquiring about u.

LIONKING: may he is jealous or suspicious.

JUNGLECAT: oh no. he is not that type of a guy. he is quite broad minded.

LIONKING: I am looking forward to meet him.

JUNGLECAT: how is Meeta?

LIONKING: like all females she is jealous of u.

JUNGLECAT: really. have u not explained our relation to her.

LIONKING: I have but even then. dont u think females r by nature more suspicious than males.

JUNGLECAT: it is bcz women r more emotional and expressive of their feelings and thus their jealousy shows, otherwise I think men r equally jealous.

LIONKING: but I am not jealous of Abhi.

JUNGLECAT: that is bcz u r in different boats.

LIONKING: r u jealous of Meeta?

JUNGLECAT: no, not at all. she is ur GF and I am ur friend.

LIONKING: but I value friends more.

JUNGLECAT: me too. I can trust u more than Abhi.

LIONKING: let us now exchange photographs.

JUNGLECAT: r u sure?

LIONKING: yes.

JUNGLECAT: ok. I will send my photographs today.

LIONKING: I will do the same.

JUNGLECAT: cant we meet soon in near future?

LIONKING: let me see if I can come over to Delhi some day.

JUNGLECAT: pl do come. it will be a great pleasure.

LIONKING: this Sunday I am busy in Green Ideas project. In fact now every Sunday I will be busy.

JUNGLECAT: u better come on a working day so that we will be able to meet in the college time.

LIONKING: no, I will meet u only if u dont hide it from anybody.

JUNGLECAT: u have misunderstood. I am not hiding anything. in fact very soon I will tell my parents about u.

LIONKING: it would make more sense to ist tell them about Abhi.

JUNGLECAT: that is tough one.

LIONKING: gather courage and do it now. dont delay it.

JUNGLECAT: but I want to clear a few things with Abhi before I finally disclose it to my parents.

LIONKING: like?

JUNGLECAT: firstly I want to know whether he is going to avail of OBC reservation if he appears 4 civil services exam.

LIONKING: that is his birth right. u cant deny it to him.

JUNGLECAT: u r right. but I have the right to know that if I marry him, what will be the status of our children. will they also belong to OBC category?

LIONKING: if he yes, then?

JUNGLECAT: I have already told u that my children would not belong to any OBC.

LIONKING: if he does not agree to that, then?

JUNGLECAT: then we r on our separate ways.

LIONKING: Radha, don't be that adamant on that issue. that can be sorted out after marriage.

JUNGLECAT: no, I am very sure that it has to be decided before we tie the knot.

LIONKING: dont take any hasty decision. give it a serious thought. let us not prejudge him. first discuss the issue with him and then take a thoughtful decision.

JUNGLECAT: thanks 4 ur advice.

LIONKING: let us call it a day on a positive note.

JUNGLECAT: ok. good night.

LIONKING: good night. take care. bye.

JUNGLECAT: bye.

19 February 2002

10 p.m.

JUNGLECAT: hi handsome.

LIONKING: hi junglee billi [wild cat].

JUNGLECAT: u r really charming.

LIONKING: r u charmed?

JUNGLECAT: yes.

LIONKING: then leave Abhi. come into my arms.

JUNGLECAT: r u serious?

LIONKING: u know I am joking. u r also really very beautiful.

JUNGLECAT: I am more beautiful than my photograph.

LIONKING: really?

JUNGLECAT: yes.

LIONKING: now I am feeling jealous of Abhi.

JUNGLECAT: and I am jealous of Meeta.

LIONKING: I am very eager to meet u.

JUNGLECAT: why this eagerness?

LIONKING: I want to shake ur beautiful hand.

JUNGLECAT: lol. u r a compulsive flirt.

LIONKING: u r my real friend to whom I can say anything and I know u wont mind and wont misunderstand me.

JUNGLECAT: I rely on u the same way.

LIONKING: how is everybody at home?

JUNGLECAT: fine. today when I was downloading ur photos, Mom was standing behind me and I did not notice her.

LIONKING: oh. what did she say?

JUNGLECAT: she was very inquisitive. and I told her about our friendship.

LIONKING: what was her reaction?

JUNGLECAT: she only asked if i was sure it was only friendship. but she liked your photo and said "the boy is handsome."

LIONKING: was she convinced?

JUNGLECAT: not exactly.

LIONKING: have u discussed the matter of your imaginary children with Abhi?

JUNGLECAT: no, not yet. Ashu cant u ist meet Abhi before I discuss the matter with him?

LIONKING: but why?

JUNGLECAT: I don't know. But I feel it would be much better if u meet him ist.

LIONKING: in my view u discuss the issue with him before I meet him. If he says no to your suggestion then there is no point in my meeting him. If he agrees to your proposal only then I will meet him.

JUNGLECAT: ok. agreed.

LIONKING: let us hope everything works out the way u want it.

JUNGLECAT: I am keeping my fingers crossed but I am very tense.

LIONKING: don't worry. everything will be fine. how is younger brother Rajan?

JUNGLECAT: he is busy in studies. wants to be a doctor.

LIONKING: good.

LIONKING: incidentally, did u talk to ur friends about doing some social work to prevent female feticide?

JUNGLECAT: yes. we r working on it. the question is who would carry on the work after we leave after 3–4 months.

LIONKING: take in some ist year students and 2–3 teachers and the chain will continue.

JUNGLECAT: u have solution 4 every problem.

LIONKING: I am doing the same for Green Ideas.

JUNGLECAT: u r very thorough.

LIONKING: my Mom has taken 26 years to make me smart & intelligent, but ur 2 months company has made me stupid.

JUNGLECAT: lol. u r stupid bcz of me and I am idiot bcz of u.

LIONKING: Ashu once upon a time u were also a very intelligent person but this JUNGLECAT has sucked all ur brains and now u r a good 4 nothing fellow.

JUNGLECAT: really?

LIONKING: yes. u came, sat in my heart, sucked my brains, made me a stupid and now gone to Abhi.

JUNGLECAT: lol. u r impossible.

LIONKING: let us relieve some of ur tensions.

JUNGLECAT: how? r u going to tell a joke?

LIONKING: Santa told Banta that he was getting a divorce.

Banta: Why?

Santa: My wife wasn't home the entire night and in the morning she said she spent the night at her sister's house. Banta: Then?

Santa: She was lying, I spent the night with her sister.

JUNGLECAT: lol. here is one from me:

A husband asks his wife" will u marry after I die?"

Wife: No, I will live with my sister. Will u marry if I die? Husband: No, I will also live with your sister.

LIONKING: lol. Radha I have some assignments to do. so let us bid good night.

JUNGLECAT: ok. good night.

LIONKING: good night. bye.

22 February 2002

9.30 p.m.

That day I was very eager to meet Radha. The project was very successful at PGIMR. As soon as I logged in to YM, I received an SMS from Radha

JUNGLECAT: hi my darling friend

LIONKING: hi

JUNGLECAT: what is up?

LIONKING: I told u not to ask this question again.

JUNGLECAT: oh sorry. I did not mean any offence.

LIONKING: but if I tell u that will be an offence on my part.

JUNGLECAT: there is one great news. I have got placement in HDFC Bank.

LIONKING: really, that is great. package?

JUNGLECAT: rupees 6 lac.

LIONKING: not bad.

JUNGLECAT: what about u?

LIONKING: as u already know I will be joining family business.

JUNGLECAT: mom was again enquiring about u?

LIONKING: like all parents she must be worried about the company u keep or she must be looking at me as a prospective son-in-law.

JUNGLECAT: may be both. how was the project in PGI?

LIONKING: it was a tremendous success. now even local news papers are lauding our efforts.

JUNGLECAT: so now u r a celebrity. let us have a treat.

LIONKING: sure.

JUNGLECAT: then come over to Delhi. I am very keen to meet u and also I want u to meet Abhi.

LIONKING: Radha u know my weekends r occupied by project work. I will have to bunk classes to come to Delhi. let me see the schedule 4 the week and see which day suits me. And of course u also would have to miss the classes.

JUNGLECAT: ok. decide by tomorrow.

LIONKING: cant I meet Abhi on the net? then if required I will meet him in person when I come to Delhi.

JUNGLECAT: will tomorrow 5pm will be ok. after college we will go to some cyber café.

LIONKING: ok. what should I discuss with him?

JUNGLECAT: u r an intelligent person, work it out.

LIONKING: I was but ur company has made me stupid.

JUNGLECAT: mr. stupid I want your well considered opinion as it is a question of my whole life.

LIONKING: ok. I will prepare a well thought out questionnaire.

JUNGLECAT: it should not look like an interview.

LIONKING: u will remain an idiot.

JUNGLECAT: u mean always.

LIONKING: yes forever.

JUNGLECAT: I think u have forgotten about my sharp teeth and big nails.

LIONKING: how can I forget what was once mine.

JUNGLECAT: lol. so tomorrow 5pm is fixed.

LIONKING: I hope everything goes fine.

JUNGLECAT: don't worry. Just be yourself.

LIONKING: ok then see u tomorrow. Just one thing, if my opinion about Abhi is negative, then ????

JUNGLECAT: then I will give my relation with Abhi a second thought.

LIONKING: ok. see u. luv.

JUNGLECAT: luv u. good night.

LIONKING: good night.

23 February 2002

5 p.m.

As soon as the last lecture was over, I rushed to my house and asked Mom to send my evening tea to my room. I switched on the PC and logged in to YM and waited for Radha and Abhi. At 5.05 p.m., I received her SMS.

JUNGLECAT: hi Ashu. how r u?

LIONKING: hi Radha. how r u?

JUNGLECAT: here meet my bf Abhi.

LIONKING: hi Abhi. how r u?

JUNGLECAT (Abhi) : fine and u?

LIONKING: great. nice to see u, I mean meet u.

JUNGLECAT (Abhi): I am also pleased to meet u. Radha has been praising u a lot and I was very eager to meet her great friend.

LIONKING: Radha has been telling me a lot about your relationship.

JUNGLECAT (Abhi): everything?

LIONKING: that only she can answer if she wishes.

JUNGLECAT: yes almost everything.

LIONKING: we r quite frank with each other.

JUNGLECAT (Abhi): she should not be that frank with a person whom she has not met in person. u must agree that here everybody is masked and u don't know what is there behind that mask.

LIONKING: u r right. we have gone through that phase but now we r real friends and r not hiding anything from each other.

JUNGLECAT (Abhi): oh really.

LIONKING: yes and Mr. Abhi if u want to tie the knot with her, u will have to get my approval ist.

JUNGLECAT (Abhi): but why? u r not her guardian.

LIONKING: right. but we have promised to get each other's approval of the match before getting married.

JUNGLECAT (Abhi): that is too much 4 a two month old relationship. even I don't have that sort of friendship with her after two years of love affair.

LIONKING: I am myself surprised at the intensity of our faith in each other.

JUNGLECAT (Abhi): Ashu I am jealous of u. I am feeling very odd.

LIONKING: it means u don't approve of our relationship.

JUNGLECAT (Abhi): frankly yes. I am not happy about the intensity of your friendship. do u luv her?

LIONKING: what if I say yes?

JUNGLECAT (Abhi): and she?

LIONKING: ask her?

JUNGLECAT: what if I say yes?

JUNGLECAT (Abhi): what sort of game u two r playing with me?

LIONKING: no game Abhi. Radha is beautiful and smart. I believe most of your classmates luv her. but that does not mean she also loves them all.

JUNGLECAT (Abhi): but she seems to luv u.

LIONKING: it means u don't have faith in her, in your luv and relationship.

JUNGLECAT (Abhi): it is not that but frankly I have been very uncomfortable about your relationship from the very beginning.

JUNGLECAT: Abhi I have told u a number of times that there is nothing beyond friendship between me and Ashu.

LIONKING: she is right. u should believe her.

JUNGLECAT (Abhi): u should not advise me, I know her more than u.

LIONKING: u r right in terms of time. but u don't seem to understand her.

JUNGLECAT (Abhi): u mean to say u understand her better.

LIONKING: cool down friend. she or we don't have to assure u time and again.

JUNGLECAT (Abhi): ok agreed that u r only good friends. Radha can u leave Ashu for me?

JUNGLECAT: that is a stupid question to ask. ok now let me ask, if I say no will u still be my BF or not.

LIONKING: no no. pl no. don't argue bcz of me. If Abhi feels comfortable without me in your life, I promise I will never meet Radha after u tie the knot with her.

JUNGLECAT (Abhi): u promise?

LIONKING: yes I do. now tell me when r u tying the knot?

JUNGLECAT (Abhi): no haste. In 2–3 months we will be finishing college. then we will see what sort of placement we get.

LIONKING: Radha was telling u wanted to get into civil services like your parents.

JUNGLECAT (Abhi): yes I am very much interested and confident of clearing the exam.

LIONKING: in general category or reserve category?

JUNGLECAT (Abhi): why do u ask that question?

LIONKING: sorry. no offence.

JUNGLECAT (Abhi): though I am confident of clearing it in general category but I would compete in reserve category bcz there chances r brighter and why not that is my birth right.

LIONKING: and after u it will be the birth right of your children.

JUNGLECAT (Abhi): what do u mean?

LIONKING: Abhi, both your parents are top officers in the Indian Govt. and enjoy all the privileges which most of us upper cast people don't have.

JUNGLECAT (Abhi): then what? they have reached this place after lot of hard work.

LIONKING: I agree but now your family is no longer backward. In fact u belong to the upper layer of the society in terms of status, privileges and wealth.

JUNGLECAT (Abhi): then what?

LIONKING: is it justified that u again declare yourself to be backward for the sake of availing the benefit of reservation.

JUNGLECAT (Abhi): that is my birth right. so it were u who misguided Radha about the reservation issue.

LIONKING: she is mature enough to judge for herself what is right or wrong. let us drop this sensitive issue.

JUNGLECAT (Abhi): thanks. what r your plans after MBA.

LIONKING: before I answer that just one more question if u don't mind.

JUNGLECAT (Abhi): just shoot.

LIONKING: do u really luv Radha?

JUNGLECAT (Abhi): that is a stupid question. of course I really luv her, she is my sweetheart.

LIONKING: but why? why not some other girl?

JUNGLECAT (Abhi): so that she can be yours.

LIONKING: not again. Just answer me what attracts u to Radha?

JUNGLECAT (Abhi): she is beautiful and I like her.

LIONKING: there r many girls who r more beautiful than Radha or if in future a more beautiful girl comes into contact with u, will u leave Radha for her.

JUNGLECAT (Abhi): never. I like her personality.

LIONKING: ok. leave it. now to answer your question I intend to join my father's pharmaceutical business.

JUNGLECAT (Abhi): u could have done that much earlier. what is the use of doing MBA?

LIONKING: doing MBA does not mean u have to join outside company. I can do that for our own company what I would be doing for some other company. more over I will be with my family throughout my life.

JUNGLECAT (Abhi): do u have a gf?

LIONKING: yes. Radha must have told u. her name is Meeta and she is a classmate.

JUNGLECAT (Abhi): do u intend to marry her?

LIONKING: yes if Radha approves and my parents agree.

JUNGLECAT (Abhi): if Radha does not approve?

LIONKING: then I won't but she will have to convince me.

JUNGLECAT (Abhi): and if your parents don't agree.

LIONKING: there is no reason for my parents to refuse. she belongs to a respectable family, is well educated, beautiful and above all I love her.

JUNGLECAT: I am getting late.

LIONKING: ok. let us call it a day.

JUNGLECAT (Abhi): what is your decision?

LIONKING: decision?

JUNGLECAT (Abhi): do u approve me as a match for Radha?

LIONKING: ist that I will tell only Radha. secondly this is an important issue and will require careful consideration.

JUNGLECAT (Abhi): ok. when r we meeting again?

LIONKING: this week I may be coming to Delhi. may be then.

JUNGLECAT (Abhi): see u then. bye for now.

LIONKING: bye. nice to meet u. bye Radha.

JUNGLECAT: bye. see u at 10.00 PM.

10 p.m.

I was thinking about the conversation I had with Abhi. Was he the right choice for Radha? I could not answer that. The reservation issue was bothering me. Maybe I had very strong views on the issue and was not in favour of any type of reservation, especially for the next generation. Otherwise, these so-called backward classes would never be able to shed the tag of OBC. In a way, Abhi was right. He was entitled to avail reservation because of his birth endorsed by the constitution or law of the land. Why should he not avail it? Simply because I was against it or Radha was against it and many more upper-caste guys were against it. We were also right in our place as guys like Abhi who belonged to the creamy layer of the society had no moral right to avail the benefit of reservation. But they had the constitutional sanction. So what was needed was to change the reservation policy. I was so engrossed in my thoughts that I did not notice the SMS from Radha till the time she buzzed me.

JUNGLECAT: hi stupid. where r u lost ?

LIONKING: hi idiot. i was thinking about Abhi.

JUNGLECAT: what?

LIONKING: this reservation issue is bothering me.

JUNGLECAT: me too.

LIONKING: how strongly do u feel about the issue?

JUNGLECAT: I don't have a scale. but I am sure about one thing, my children wont belong to an OBC family.

LIONKING: and what about Abhi. r u in favour of Abhi availing the benefits of OBC ?

JUNGLECAT: on moral grounds he should not. but we cant deny him his legal right.

LIONKING: but u r denying the same right to your would be children.

JUNGLECAT: I can do that bcz they will be known by my sir name.

LIONKING: they may be known by your sir name but by birth they will still belong to OBC.

JUNGLECAT: then what is the solution?

LIONKING: Abhi will have to drop his OBC tag.

JUNGLECAT: but it looks he wont and his parents wont let him do that.

LIONKING: this all boils down to one thing : how strongly u feel about the issue? can u ignore the implications of marrying an OBC man for the sake of your luv 4 him?

JUNGLECAT: I am very confused Ashu. pl guide me.

LIONKING: no I cant guide u in this matter. It will be your personal decision. no haste, just think patiently and then take a well thought out decision. after all this is a question of your whole life.

JUNGLECAT: u r right. let me consider the whole issue without my emotions clouding my judgment.

LIONKING: don't worry. I know u r a fool but not an emotional one.

JUNGLECAT: Ashu pl be serious. this is a question of my whole life.

LIONKING: so be patient. there is no haste. give it time and thought.

JUNGLECAT: so u r coming to Delhi this week?

LIONKING: do u have an off day on Saturday?

JUNGLECAT: yes. but

LIONKING: cant I come on Saturday and have lunch with your family.

JUNGLECAT: I am not sure. I will be delighted but i have to talk to my parents.

LIONKING: ok then. If your parents say yes.

LIONKING: what did Abhi said about me?

JUNGLECAT: nothing much. but he did not seem to be happy about our relationship.

LIONKING: I think he is still suspicious and jealous also.

JUNGLECAT: may be but he was happy to meet u. what is your opinion about him?

LIONKING: I don't want to say anything now. let me ist meet him then I will let u know.

JUNGLECAT: as u wish.

LIONKING: can u mail me his photograph.

JUNGLECAT: I will do it tomorrow.

LIONKING: ok. bye now.

JUNGLECAT: bye. good night.

LIONKING: good night. sweet dreams.

24 February 2002

I had received Abhi's photographs. He looked to be handsome and smart and was a perfect match for Radha. But marriages don't last solely on the basis of looks. Both hearts should also meet. Though legally it is an agreement between two people but for the agreement to succeed both should love each other and above all should be good friends otherwise it becomes an arrangement. I was worried for Radha as somewhere in my heart I had a feeling that her marriage with Abhi won't work because of two things. Firstly they came from different social backgrounds. Secondly Radha did not seem to be very interested in power and authority associated with highly placed government officers. She was a very sensitive and emotional girl who had above-average social values whereas Abhi had been brought up amidst authority and privileges which come with high government position, and he must have become used to it. And if he was to become a Indian civil services officer, which he intended to do, he might become more arrogant which will be a disaster for their marriage. Further Radha looked to be quite beautiful from her photograph, so Abhi might be just infatuated by her beauty, and he might not be truly in love with her. How could I get answers to these questions? Maybe Radha herself would provide the answers. I will put these questions before Radha and then ask her to judge for herself on the basis of her feelings and Abhi's behaviour.

It was five minutes past 10 p.m., and I was not logged in to YM. I immediately logged in to YM, and Radha was upon me like a hungry cat.

JUNGLECAT: hi. where were u?

LIONKING: thinking about u and Abhi.

JUNGLECAT: there is a bad news.

LIONKING: your parents have not agreed for my lunch.

JUNGLECAT: yes.

LIONKING: then ask them for evening tea.

JUNGLECAT: stupid.

LIONKING: I am not that stupid that u can make a fool of me. I know u and through u your parents. they cant have any objection.

JUNGLECAT: why r u so confident?

LIONKING: parents of every young girl r on the lookout for a decent boy who is suitable to be their son-in-law. so they will happily welcome such a guy in their house.

JUNGLECAT: u r a good analyst of human behavior.

JUNGLECAT: ok. they have agreed. what will be the program like?

LIONKING: I will reach your house by 12.00 noon and after that I will be at your mercy.

JUNGLECAT: no your honor, u will be my guest of honor. what would u like to have 4 lunch?

LIONKING: you.

JUNGLECAT: should I cook myself?

LIONKING: no rather I would enjoy eating u raw.

JUNGLECAT: lol. pl tell me what would u like to have in lunch.

LIONKING: anything u cook with your beautiful hands.

JUNGLECAT: that is a long tough order. I will prepare one dish 4 u, the rest of the cooking will be done by Mom.

LIONKING: ok. put all your luv in that one dish.

JUNGLECAT: sure. and after lunch?

LIONKING: we shall have coffee in some nearby café and tell Abhi to meet us there at about 4.00 PM. I must leave for Chandigarh by 5.00PM.

JUNGLECAT: but we will get very little time to ourselves.

LIONKING: Radha it will take 5 hours to reach Chandigarh. we will spend more time alone when we meet next.

JUNGLECAT: promise.

LIONKING: promise.

JUNGLECAT: how do u like Abhi's pics.

LIONKING: he looks to be smart and handsome. how big is he?

JUNGLECAT: u naughty. I have not seen nor have I asked Abhi.

LIONKING: lol. idiot I mean his height and weight.

JUNGLECAT: 5'8", and he must be weighing around 65 kg. wheatish complexion.

LIONKING: good.

JUNGLECAT: I am very excited about our meeting.

LIONKING: me too. should I bring any gift 4 u or your parents.

JUNGLECAT: I don't know about my parents but 4 me bring that monkey cap u brought from SHIMLA 4 me.

LIONKING: u have not forgotten. should I bring a small bouquet 4 your parents.

JUNGLECAT: that would be perfect.

LIONKING: ok. then see u tomorrow.

JUNGLECAT: ok. bye. luv u.

LIONKING: bye. good night.

JUNGLECAT: good night.

5

FIRST MEETING

27 February 2002

I left for Delhi early in the morning in my own car. I had breakfast at a roadside dhaba at Murthal. These dhabas serve really nice food and lots of people stop there to have breakfast, lunch, and dinner.

I reached Delhi at 11 a.m. and Lajpat Nagar, the locality where Radha lived, at about 11.45 a.m. It took me another ten to fifteen minutes to find the house, and at exactly 12 noon I rang her doorbell. It was immediately opened by Radha as if she was waiting by the door side. We hugged each other and shook hands and stood there looking at each other. It was a magic moment. She was looking stunning in a yellow suit, more beautiful than I had imagined. Instinctively I took her hand and kissed it. She turned red, and at that very moment, her mom called. We went inside, and I bid namaste (respectful greetings) to her mom and presented her a bouquet of roses. She was around fifty years old and still looked very beautiful. Then Radha introduced me to her younger brother, Rajan. We settled on the sofas in the living room, and tea was served with snacks.

Radha was beaming; she seemed to be very pleased to see me in person. Her mom enquired about my family, my papa's business, and my future plans as if she was interviewing a would-be son-in-law. Radha's dad was not there; he had gone to the office for some important work. Then Radha showed me the rest of the house and then took me to her room. I sat on a chair and she on her bed, and we looked into each others' eyes for a long time. Then she broke the silence.

'How was the journey?' she enquired.

'Oh, it was very boring. But thoughts of meeting you kept me occupied,' I replied.

Radha: You must have started quite early.

Me: Yes, at about 6.30 a.m.

Radha: Did you eat anything on your way? You must be feeling hungry?

Me: I had breakfast at Murthal. I am feeling OK. You are looking very beautiful.

Radha: Mister, I am not looking beautiful, but I am beautiful. Incidentally, you are also looking very handsome.

Me: Madam, for your information, I was born handsome. Here is your cap, you will look really yourself in this cap.

Radha: Thanks. Can I try it right now?

She put it on, and we both started laughing. At that moment, her mom came in, and she also started laughing.

Me: Auntie, Radha is looking very cute in this cap.

Mrs Malhotra: She is looking like herself. Very naughty.

Me: Auntie, that is what I told her.

At this, Radha started making faces.

Mrs Malhotra: Radha, your papa won't be able to join us. Should I serve the lunch?

Radha: Mom, may I help?

Mrs Malhotra: No, no. You must give Ashu company. I will call you when food is served.

And she left the room. Radha, in a mock fight, started beating me.

Radha: You called me a monkey.

Me: No. You are a junglee billi [cat].

Radha: With long nails and sharp teeth.

We both started laughing. She took off the cap and combed her hair.

Me: You have nice hair. Long and shiny.

Radha: I specially shampooed them twice today for you.

Me: So you wanted to look beautiful to me.

Radha: I also applied fresh matching nail polish.

And she showed her nails as if to bite me.

Me: What else did you do to impress me?

Radha: Applied mascara to my eyelashes. Have I impressed you?

Me: You have killed me.

Radha: You are a compulsive flirt.

Me: How will Abhi feel if he hears our conversation.

Radha: Do you care?

Me: No. Why should I? My conscience is clear.

At that very moment, her mom called for lunch.

Me: Which is the dish you have prepared?

Radha: Myself.

Me: Tujhe to mein kisi din kachcha hi khaoonga [I will eat you raw someday].

Radha: I will be waiting for that day. For today, I have prepared malai kofta for you.

During lunch I discussed films with Rajan and enquired about his future plans. The food was really delicious.

Me: Auntie, the food is very tasty.

Radha: I also deserve some praise.

Me: I forgot. Radha, the vegetables are really nicely chopped.

Radha: Ashu, I will kill you.

Me: Auntie, this malai kofta is out of this world, fit for the aliens.

Radha: Mom, tell him to shut up, otherwise I will not talk to him.

And everybody had a hearty laugh. Radha was behaving like a small child, and I liked her childish behaviour with amusement.

Mrs Malhotra: Ashu, will you have some coffee.

Me: No, thank you, Auntie. Actually I have to do some shopping, and we shall have coffee in the market. Auntie, please do come to Chandigarh someday.

Mrs Malhotra: My elder sister lives in Chandigarh, and her son is to be married soon. Maybe then I will come to bless the couple.

Me: Auntie, please do visit us then. My parents shall be very delighted to meet you. And thank you, Auntie, for the nice food.

I bade goodbye to Auntie and Rajan and left the house along with Radha. As planned, we went to the nearby market and settled ourselves at a corner table in the cafe. The time was 3 p.m., and Abhi was expected at 4 p.m., so we had one full hour to ourselves.

Radha: What do you want to shop?

Me: Nothing.

Radha: I thought you are buying me a gift.

Me: Should I?

Radha: Your choice.

Me: What would you like to have?

Radha: A bucket full of popcorn.

We both laughed, and I ordered a bucket of popcorn and two cups of coffee.

Radha: What do you plan to discuss with Abhi?

Me: Radha, I think the reservation issue has been discussed, and the rest is to be discussed between you and him.

Radha: Right. I will do it very soon. Maybe today itself after you leave.

Me: The other thing I want to see is whether he really loves you or he is just infatuated by your beauty.

Radha: How will you do it?

Me: I don't know. I have been thinking. What do you suggest?

Radha: If you ask him directly, he will definitely say that he loved me from the core of his heart.

Me: Surely. I have an idea, but I will have to feed him some lies.

The coffee had arrived with popcorn which I presented to her with a smile, and she accepted it as if it was the most costly gift she had ever received.

Radha: What do you have in mind?

Me: What sort of dress does Abhi's mom wear?

Radha: She always wears a sari, and I suppose, in his family, all ladies are supposed to wear sari.

Me: And what is your favourite dress?

Radha: Punjabi suit or jeans and T-shirt.

Me: Has Abhi ever seen you in a sari?

Radha: I have never worn a sari in my life, and I don't think I will feel comfortable in a sari.

Me: OK then. Let me try this one.

At that moment, Radha waved to somebody who was entering the cafe. It was Abhi. Abhi approached our table, and we said hello to each other and shook hands, and he settled into a chair opposite me.

Me: Nice to see you. What will you have? We are having coffee.

Abhi: Same for me.

Radha: Have you taken lunch?

Abhi: Yes. And you?

Radha: Yes. Me and Ashu had lunch at my house.

Abhi: That is very unfair. You should have invited me also.

Radha: Sorry. Some other time.

Abhi: You are looking very beautiful in this suit. The colour suits you very well.

Radha : Thanks.

The opening was there, and I immediately snatched it.

Me: Radha, what is your favourite dress?

    She stared at me as if trying to understand why I was asking this question as she had already told me about her dress preferences. I winked at her.

Radha: Punjabi suit and jeans and T-shirt.

Me: Have you ever tried a sari?

She again looked at me as if I were an idiot.

Radha: No, never. I don't like sari.

Abhi: But, Radha, if you become my wife, you have to wear saris as in our family all the ladies wear saris.

Me: But she can't wear a sari.

Abhi: Why not?

Me: Because she. Radha, you have not told him?

Radha: What?

Me: That you have a big burn mark on your tummy.

She looked at me strangely and then nodded slightly to indicate that she understood the trick.

Radha: No. I had thought of telling him about it only when we had agreed to tie the knot.

Abhi: So that is the reason why you can't wear a sari, because that burn mark will be exposed. You should have told me that much earlier.

Radha: I did not tell you earlier because I was planning to have plastic surgery done for that ugly mark.

Abhi: How did it happen?

Radha: When I was about ten years, my mom was frying something in the kitchen, and I came from behind, and she accidentally hit the frying pan, spilling the boiling oil, and some of it fell on my abdomen.

Me: Awful.

Abhi: Very sorry. But you should not have hidden it from me. It means Ashu is more close to you than me.

Radha: It is not that. I was—

Abhi: No, you intended to hide it from me. You were cheating.

Radha: Abhi, I never intended to cheat you or hide it from you. Just think how long could I hide it from you.

Abhi: Whatever, I am not happy about it.

I had done the job. In the next few days, everything will become clear. If he really loved Radha, he will ignore the burn mark and accept her. If he was only infatuated by her beauty, he will start distancing himself from Radha. I thought it better to leave them alone. For some time we sat there in silence each drowned in his or her own thoughts.

Me: It is already 5 p.m., and I am getting late. So I will take your leave now.

The atmosphere was very tense. So neither of them replied. I got up and shook hands with both of them.

Me: Nice meeting you, Abhi. Please do come to Chandigarh someday. Radha, take care.

I winked at Radha, and she nodded and I left the cafe.

6

THE GIRLFRIEND

28 February 2002

I was very tired as that Sunday we had covered Rose Garden, Rock Garden, and Sukhna Lake for the clean Chandigarh project. However, I was very keen to meet Radha to know what happened between her and Abhi after I left Delhi.

I was thinking whether I had done the right thing by feeding Abhi a lie. I was feeling guilty because it was due to my lie that he had called Radha a cheat. But I could not think of any other way to judge whether his love for Radha was true or it was pure infatuation. I logged in to YM and immediately got a message from Radha.

JUNGLECAT: hi. how r u?

LIONKING: very tired.

JUNGLECAT: bcz of the project? was it a success?

LIONKING: yes. today even the tourists participated. what happened after I left?

JUNGLECAT: I felt sorry for not telling him about the burn mark at the very outset but he was adamant and kept on accusing me of cheating.

LIONKING: I am very sorry. I am feeling guilty. It is bcz of my lie that u have to tolerate these insults.

JUNGLECAT: no need to feel guilty after all it was 4 my wellbeing. your idea was brilliant.

LIONKING: let us hope it works for the good. I hope he will excuse u and accept u with that burn mark.

JUNGLECAT: I don't think so. he was so irritated.

LIONKING: may be it was bcz you had told me about it before telling him and he was feeling left out or neglected. Jealousy.

JUNGLECAT: whatever but he was feeling very bad about it.

LIONKING: tomorrow when you meet him you will get some idea about his feelings.

JUNGLECAT: Ashu I am very anxious and worried.

LIONKING: don't worry everything will be fine. did auntie say anything about me.

JUNGLECAT: yes, she was praising u a lot. smart, intelligent, well mannered and what not.

LIONKING: I know what she was thinking.

JUNGLECAT: what?

LIONKING: that her idiot daughter had found a perfect son-in-law for her.

JUNGLECAT: yes that is what she was telling my Dad.

LIONKING: u should clarify to them before it is too late.

JUNGLECAT: I have already done that. but she was not convinced. was Meeta with you for the project work?

LIONKING: yes. she was there all the time.

JUNGLECAT: when will you introduce her to me?

LIONKING: whenever u say.

JUNGLECAT: tomorrow I will be back from college by 5.00PM. Incidentally what have u told Meeta about me.

LIONKING: just that we r good friends. that u r a real beauty. that u r smart and I have not told her that u r an idiot.

JUNGLECAT: lol. is she jealous of me.

LIONKING: must be. suspicion and jealousy r birth right of u ladies.

JUNGLECAT: I am feeling very jittery at the thought of meeting your gf.

LIONKING: then don't meet. It was your desire.

JUNGLECAT: will u tie the knot without my approval?

LIONKING: no never. one day u have to meet her, so why not now.

JUNGLECAT: ok. I am ready.

LIONKING: ok. tomorrow 5.30 PM. now I must rest. I am dead tired.

JUNGLECAT: ok. bye. good night and sweet dreams.

LIONKING: bye. incidentally I must tell u that u r a stunning beauty.

JUNGLECAT: thanks. bye. c u.

LIONKING: c u.

1 March, 5.30 p.m.

I took Meeta to the cybercafe in the university market. We took two computers and logged in to YM. Radha was already there.

JUNGLECAT: hi your majesty.

LIONKING: hi beauty. Meeta is with me.

JUNGLECAT: hi Meeta.

LIONKING: no no. she will be logging in from another computer with her own id- MEETA4U.

JUNGLECAT: but how the three of us will chat together.

LIONKING: u can open up a new room here. make it public or private and control the access of other people to that room. only invitees can enter the room.

JUNGLECAT: oh really. that is very nice arrangement.

LIONKING: just a minute, here she is. give me a minute to brief her. when I invite u to the private room, just accept the invitation.

JUNGLECAT: ok. but u have to promise that u will not rape me there.

LIONKING: lol. idiot.

I created a new room and invited both JUNGLECAT and MEETA4U.

JUNGLECAT was the first to join.

LIONKING: I hope u did not face any problem on way to this room.

JUNGLECAT: no Your Majesty. the journey was pleasant. thx for inviting me to the party.

LIONKING: it is my pleasure to have a distinguished personality like u as my guest. be comfortable. have a seat.

JUNGLECAT: thx Your Majesty.

At that moment, MEETA4U entered the room.

LIONKING: hi Meeta. here meet my new friend Junglecat.

JUNGLECAT: hi Meeta. nice to meet u.

MEETA4U: hi Junglecat. Ashu told me u r a very interesting personality.

JUNGLECAT: it is his opinion. u may not endorse it.

MEETA4U: let us see. so u r also doing MBA. which college?

JUNGLECAT: Faculty of Management Studies, Delhi

MEETA4U: how r u in studies?

JUNGLECAT: just ok. not top class.

MEETA4U: but I always top my class. all four A grades.

Meeta was trying to be one up.

MEETA4U: Junglecat what r u wearing?

JUNGLECAT: u can call me Radha.

MEETA4U: yes Ashu told me that is your real name. old fashioned.

Again trying to downgrade Radha.

JUNGLECAT: winter is no time for fashion. I am at home and wearing a high neck pullover of sea green color.

MEETA4U: I hate that color. I am wearing black trousers and dark brown coat. Blackberry make. The set cost 15000 rupees.

JUNGLECAT: wow. that is too costly. ur dad must be very rich.

Radha was inflating her.

MEETA4U: yes. he is an industrialist. Hosiery goods manufacturing and export.

MEETA4U: do u have a car? how do u go to college?.

JUNGLECAT: I have Honda Activa scooter.

MEETA4U: scooty.

She was sort of insulting Radha. I hoped Radha would keep her cool.

MEETA4U: my father drives Honda City, I have my own Maruti 800 and one more car for my Mom.

JUNGLECAT: my Papa has Maruti Zen and I sometimes borrow it from him.

Radha was lying. Her father had Hyundai Accent. She was trying to satisfy Meeta's ego. Meeta was behaving strangely. Maybe she was too jealous.

MEETA4U: do u wear real or artificial jewelry? I have solitaire ear rings which Papa gave me as a birthday gift last year. u know the price. half a million rupees.

JUNGLECAT: wow. u have real class. I only wear artificial jewelry.

It was enough. Meeta was again downgrading Radha. I did not know she was so arrogant.

JUNGLECAT: do u watch TV.

MEETA4U: yes but not regularly. u know I am staying in a hostel.

JUNGLECAT: do u watch KBC.

MEETA4U; no, that does not interest me. I like watching soaps like Kahani Ghar Ghar Ki [*Story of Each Household*] and Kyunki Saas Bhi Kabhi Bahu Thi [*Because Mother-in-Law Was Once a Daughter-in-Law*]

That was typical ladies preference.

JUNGLECAT: what r ur plans 4 the future?

MEETA4U: after completing MBA, Papa will get me a job in some reputed company. he has very good links. Alternatively I will join Papa's firm as a financial analyst. and then marriage with Ashu.

LIONKING: I have not proposed u yet. further Radha has not approved u.

MEETA4U: why do I need her approval? who is she to u?

LIONKING: she is my best friend. and to tie the knot with me u have to be approved by her.

MEETA4U: she is never going to do that. she may be herself interested in u.

LIONKING: Meeta trust me. we r only good friends.

MEETA4U: it may be friendship from your side. but she may be planning to snatch u from me.

JUNGLECAT: Meeta I don't have to do that. I have a bf.

MEETA4U: oh. then it is ok, does he know about Ashu.

LIONKING: yes and in fact we have met in person.

JUNGLECAT: did u see the headlines in today's news papers.

MEETA4U: no. news papers don't interest me. I read only some selected magazines like Filmfare, Stardust and Fashion Weekly.

JUNGLECAT: do u see movies?

MEETA4U: yes regularly, but only English movies.

She was lying. She had seen many Hindi movies with me. Perhaps she was
trying to impress Radha.

JUNGLECAT: which is the latest u have seen?

MEETA4U: that one. what was its name? yes 'King of the Ring'.

JUNGLECAT: Lord of the Rings. Did u like it?

MEETA4U: no it was very boring.

Again lying. She had not seen the movie but heard about it from me.

JUNGLECAT: which color nail polish do u like?

MEETA4U: I always use matching nail polish.

JUNGLECAT: really. what is ur favorite color for lip stick?.

MEETA4U: I like glamorous colors. Bright red and flashy pink.

Why was Radha asking such meaningless questions? Perhaps she was trying to
judge her overall personality.

MEETA4U: r u beautiful?

JUNGLECAT: just average looking. how about u?

Now Radha was lying.

MEETA4U: Ashu must have told u. I am very beautiful. in college I was
College Beauty Queen.

JUNGLECAT: really. that is why Ashu is so smitten by u.

MEETA4U: r u jealous?

JUNGLECAT: no. not at all. I wish u both best of luck.

Meeta was beautiful, but she was no match to Radha.

MEETA4U: do u luv Ashu?

I was taken aback by her blunt question.

JUNGLECAT: no. as already clarified we r just friends. why ask it again?.

MEETA4U: does he loves u?

JUNGLECAT: better u ask him. suppose he loves me, then?

MEETA4U: I will kill u both.

LIONKING: Meeta u don't trust us. u have no faith in our relationship. this is height of suspicion.

Radha had fallen silent. Perhaps she was not pleased by Meeta's behaviour.

JUNGLECAT: no problem. nice meeting u Meeta.

MEETA4U: frankly I am not very pleased to meet u.

That was height of uncivilized behaviour.

LIONKING: what has happened to u Meeta. u r insulting Radha. I am sorry Radha. c u at the usual time.

Radha left the room. After that I had a bitter fight with Meeta. Her behaviour today suited an egoist, a dumbbell, an ill-mannered, uncivilized, and unpolished lady, a self-indulgent boaster. Radha would never approve her. In fact I myself was feeling ashamed. What would Radha think of my choice? But I had never seen this side of Meeta. She was really awful. And moreover she had no regrets about her behaviour.

I asked her to apologize to Radha, but she refused. I warned her that if Radha did not approve her, I would never marry her and our relationship will be over. She replied, 'Ashu, you will leave me for that slut, a girl of no class.' I raised my hand as if to slap her but controlled myself and left the scene in a rage. I was feeling as if Meeta had slapped me. I was regretting my choice of a life partner. How could she behave so cheaply? For a moment, it seemed everything was over between us.

7

THE BREAKUPS

9.30 p.m.

I was very restless. I was feeling insulted and downgraded as if Meeta had not misbehaved with Radha but me. I was feeling very awkward to face Radha. I logged in to YM before time. Radha was not yet there. I waited for her to log in, and after five minutes, I received her SMS.

JUNGLECAT: hi there.

LIONKING: hi. how r u feeling? must be feeling very bad. I am really very sorry.

JUNGLECAT: why should u feel sorry ? I am not upset.

LIONKING: I am myself surprised and ashamed at Meeta's behavior. she has always been civilized and cultured. but today she crossed all limits of indecency.

JUNGLECAT: maybe she is too suspicious and jealous.

LIONKING: whatever. her behavior today is unpardonable.

JUNGLECAT: no no. don't feel that bad. being a female I can understand her jealousy and bitterness.

LIONKING: after u left I asked her to apologize to u, but she instead of regretting, accused u and used very filthy language 4 u which I could not tolerate and was about to slap her but controlled myself.

JUNGLECAT: oh my God. It has gone that far. I am feeling guilty.

LIONKING: no, u should not. In a way I am happy it has happened now. just imagine my plight if I had to tolerate such an arrogant wife for the whole of my life.

JUNGLECAT: what do u mean?

LIONKING: I mean what u have guessed. It is all over.

JUNGLECAT: Ashu don't take such an important decision when u r upset. Just cool down and give it some time and thought.

LIONKING: may be u r right. but I cant tolerate anyone insulting u?

JUNGLECAT: but u cant sacrifice your luv for the sake of a friend.

LIONKING: yes I can bcz it is a question of right and wrong. if she is not respecting or tolerating my friends now, how will she do that after she ties the knot with me.

JUNGLECAT: don't draw hasty conclusions. Just be cool and discuss the issues with her.

LIONKING: look Radha. me and Meeta love or I should say loved each other. It is matter of heart and not mind and it has to be decided by heart.

JUNGLECAT: pl don't do it for me.

LIONKING: no, u should not feel guilty. but u should be happy and u should congratulate yourself for saving a true friend from the misery which he would have to suffer his whole life.

JUNGLECAT: u may be right but I still feel very awkward.

LIONKING: would u recommend her as my life partner?

JUNGLECAT: frankly no, never.

LIONKING: then don't feel guity. let it happen. whatever is happening is good for everyone.

JUNGLECAT: still I request u to give it a cool mind and reconsider your decision.

LIONKING: ok. did u see Abhi today?

JUNGLECAT: today I am not in a mood to discuss Abhi. let it be tomorrow.

LIONKING: ok. I again feel sorry.

JUNGLECAT: no, don't. bye for today.

LIONKING: bye. good night.

JUNGLECAT: good night. take care.

2 March 2002

Next day I went to college with a bad taste in my mouth. I detested meeting Meeta, but I knew she would not leave me that easily. As I was approaching the college gate, Meeta appeared from nowhere as if she was waiting for me. She felt sorry and asked me to meet her during recess.

In the recess, we sat at the lawns in front of the college canteen and ordered tea and samosas. I was feeling very strange and awkward as if I were meeting Meeta for the first time. Meeta was not able to meet my gaze and was looking down. She again felt sorry and apologized for her behaviour.

'But why did you behave like that? You had no right to insult my friend,' I insisted.

'I had no intention of insulting her. But I could not control myself. Ashu, I can't share you with any other girl,' she tried to justify her behaviour.

'Where was the question of sharing? She is just a good friend like any other male friend. A boy and a girl can also be good friends without any affair,' I argued.

'I am feeling very nervous as you have come very close to Radha during a short period,' she expressed her suspicion.

'You could have discussed the matter with me in private before meeting and insulting Radha,' I tried to reason with her.

'Ashu, I have said sorry. Now leave it,' she tried to dismiss the matter.

'Meeta, this is not a small matter. This incident very badly reflects on your character and nature. This can happen again in the future with any of my other friends. I can't afford to lose my friends because of your bad manners and temper,' I insisted.

She started shedding tears, which I believed to be crocodile tears, the ultimate weapon of a lady.

'Meeta, the truth is you have no faith in me. You are being too suspicious and insecure which can be disastrous for a lifelong relationship.' Her tears had no effect on me.

'What do you want, that I should touch Radha's feet and beg her forgiveness? I will do that also for you, but then you will break your relationship with her,' she offered irritably.

'Meeta, love can't coexist with conditions. Foundations of a lifelong relationship like marriage can't be based on preconditions and compromises. After marriage you have no choice but to make all sorts of compromises and adjustments. But not before tying the knot,' I tried to make her understand.

'Ashu, I have not asked you for anything. I want just your love. Nothing more.' She again started weeping.

'Meeta, love begets love. There is no place for hate. Radha did not say anything bad to you, but it looks like you hate her that is why you tried to belittle her,' I argued.

'I will never do that again,' she promised.

'How can I forget the language you used for Radha, a slut, a filthy girl. It is disgusting. How uncivilized? And for your kind information, Radha is more beautiful than you,' I stressed.

'That is why you are so smitten by her that you are prepared to break our two-year-old relationship. Why are you sitting here with me? Go sleep in her lap.' She again started weeping.

'Meeta, that is enough. You are again at it. I can't tolerate it anymore. It is all over between us. Henceforth, if you wish we can be friends, no more.' I sort of conveyed my decision.

At this she got up and started shouting at me, 'No, I don't need your friendship. You are a bastard. Go to hell.' And she ran away towards the college building.

I sat there for some time, stunned by her outburst. I was not in a mood to attend the next lecture, so I returned home and went straight to my room and lay down on the bed and started weeping like a child. It was really hurting to break away from Meeta like that.

I don't know when I fell asleep; it was 8 p.m. and Mom was waking me.

'When did you come back from college? Are you all right? Your eyes are red, it looks like you have been weeping,' Mom asked, sitting on the bed and running her hand through my hair.

'Mom, it is all over with Meeta.' I told her briefly what had happened, and in the process, I told her about Radha and my visit to her place also. Mom was also surprised by Meeta's arrogance, but she understood and endorsed my decision. I was relieved a bit and went downstairs with Mom, and we had a quiet dinner.

I was at peace now and wanted to talk to Radha. But it was only 9 p.m. I logged in to YM, and to my surprise, Radha was already logged in.

LIONKING: Hello sweet heart.

JUNGLECAT: hello. what is up today?

LIONKING: nothing. I am down and down. It is all over with Meeta.

JUNGLECAT: oh no. did u meet her today.

LIONKING: yes we had a long discussion and in the end decided to break up.

JUNGLECAT: was it a joint decision or one sided?

LIONKING: when after discussions, I found no change in her attitude I told her it would be better 4 both of us if we part ways.

JUNGLECAT: and she agreed?

LIONKING: no she was furious and abused both of us and left.

JUNGLECAT: why me?

LIONKING: bcz she thinks I am ditching her 4 u.

JUNGLECAT: u must have explained.

LIONKING: not once but time and again I tried to explain our relationship to her, but she had closed all doors of her empty brain and was not ready to listen to any reasoning.

JUNGLECAT: I am really sorry. u must be feeling very awful.

LIONKING: yes I was and wept like a child but then I talked to Mom and told her everything and she consoled me and endorsed my decision. now I am feeling better.

JUNGLECAT: did u tell her about our friendship?

LIONKING: yes everything and she understood the whole situation.

JUNGLECAT: oh dear. I am really concerned for u. don't take it to heart. I know it will be difficult but u r a brave guy of real values and character.

LIONKING: I wish u were with me.

JUNGLECAT: I myself want the same but u know it is not possible, I will try to be online 4 as much time as u desire.

LIONKING: thanks. that is very nice of u. did u meet Abhi?

JUNGLECAT: humm. no. he did not attend college today.

LIONKING: u r not lying.

JUNGLECAT: no no. why should I lie.

LIONKING: Radha do u think I have taken the right decision?

JUNGLECAT: what do u think?

LIONKING: I think I did the right thing. In a way I feel relieved when I think about the consequences if what happened now would have happened after tying the knot with her.

JUNGLECAT: then nothing else matters. in matters of heart u yourself r the best judge.

LIONKING: I know but if u were in my place what would have been your decision?

JUNGLECAT: that is a difficult one but I will be truthful. Meeta was not the right girl 4 u, so forget her and move ahead in life as if nothing bad has happened.

LIONKING: thanks Radha. that is like a true friend. I wish nothing of the sort happens between u and Abhi. I hope Abhi will pass the test and accept u with your non-existent burn marks.

JUNGLECAT:

LIONKING: Radha r u there?

JUNGLECAT: let us hope so.

LIONKING: I am feeling better now. u can make me much better if u send me a flying kiss.

JUNGLECAT: anything 4 u dear. here it comes.

LIONKING: it was sooooooooooo sweet.

JUNGLECAT: u flirt. Ok. sleep well and forget everything else.

LIONKING: promise u will come in my dreams.

JUNGLECAT: no I will come in my panties. I don't want to spoil your beautiful dreams.

LIONKING: u naughty.

JUNGLECAT: bye. good night. take care.

LIONKING: bye. good night.

3 March 2002

I slept well, and Radha did come into my dreams. She was sitting before me in a chair and was staring at me without saying anything. There were tears in her eyes. Then she got up and sat beside me and placed her hand on mine and smiled and then she was gone. I opened my eyes and found my mom kneeling over me and kissing my forehead.

'Are you all right, Ashu? Did you sleep well?' she asked with concern and affection.

'Yes, Mom. I am all right. After talking to you and then to Radha, I am feeling much better,' I replied and got up from the bed to get ready for the college.

'Ashu, don't take anything to heart and forget everything. Just ignore Meeta and keep yourself busy with studies and friends,' Mom advised.

'Right, Mom. Don't worry, I will get over it very soon,' I assured her and went into the bathroom.

That day I totally ignored Meeta and kept a distance from her. Just once in the recess we crossed each other, and I said hello to her but she did not reply. I was back from college quite early, and after resting for a while, I called for tea and biscuits and logged in to YM, hoping to find Radha. It was only 6 p.m., and there was no chance of her being online. But I still hoped. Chatting with her gave me a lot of comfort and courage. Radha was there but did not respond to my SMS. I buzzed her but still there was no reply. Maybe after logging in, she did not find me and got busy in something else. So I waited for her SMS. It came after ten minutes.

JUNGLECAT: hey. nice surprise.

LIONKING: u did not expect me to be online. then why r u there?

JUNGLECAT: I wanted to be nearby, so that u wont have to wait. how r u
      feeling?

LIONKING: much better and relaxed.

JUNGLECAT: did u meet Meeta?

LIONKING: no. I just saw her once and said hello but she did not reply.

JUNGLECAT: egoist. just leave her alone.

A gf sent a SMS to her ex bf to return her photos as she had found a new bf.
      The bf sent her 30 photos with a note to find her photo from the lot
      as he had forgotten how she looked.

LIONKING: I will try. no I will definitely do it.

JUNGLECAT: that is the spirit. Be always cheerful.

LIONKING: what about Abhi, did u see him?

JUNGLECAT: leave it. we shall discuss it some other day.

LIONKING: what is the matter Radha? u r avoiding the issue.

JUNGLECAT: 😢 😢 😢

LIONKING: why r u weeping? what happened?

JUNGLECAT: it seems to be over.

LIONKING: what happened?

JUNGLECAT: we have met twice but all the time he is accusing me of cheating.

JUNGLECAT: I told him that I intended to tell him when he proposed but he is not ready to listen.

JUNGLECAT: I told him that I will immediately go for plastic surgery, but he is not listening to any reasoning.

LIONKING: oh my God. I did not think it will lead to this.

JUNGLECAT: when I persisted and even apologized 4 the lapse, do u know what he said.

LIONKING: what?

JUNGLECAT: he said why should he compromise. I even asked what if I had got these burn marks after marriage.

LIONKING: what did he say?

JUNGLECAT: he said that would be another matter. but now since nothing has been formalized, why should he compromise when he could find another more beautiful girl.

LIONKING: that is awful. so his only criterion 4 a suitable match is beauty.

JUNGLECAT: it looks like that.

LIONKING: I am sorry. what now? Radha u can still tell him the truth.

JUNGLECAT: no Ashu. I had to find his true feelings about me. now nothing more. we have amicably parted ways. no bitterness. we shall remain friends.

LIONKING: oh dear. u must be an emotional mess. And u were so concerned about me. u were trying to cheer me up.

JUNGLECAT: Ashu in a way whatever has happened is for the good of everybody. he did not loved Radha's soul but her lovely face, her beautiful body only.

LIONKING: but still it must be hurting a lot. I know it is not easy to break a relation.

JUNGLECAT: I will get over it very soon. I need only your support. In fact we need each others' help.

LIONKING: why this had to happen to both of us at the same time. do u think our friendship is in any way responsible 4 the breakups.

JUNGLECAT: may be. but we r not at fault. our conscience is clear. In a way we have been saved from future disasters.

LIONKING: u r right. try to get over it asap.

JUNGLECAT: we shall cheer up each other and soon we will get over it.

LIONKING: will u be my friend 4 ever?.

JUNGLECAT: that is cute. I promise I will be your best friend 4 ever.

LIONKING: bye for now. r we meeting at 10.00 PM.

JUNGLECAT: yes. eat well. save some ice cream 4 me.

LIONKING: sure. c u.

8

JOINING BROKEN HEARTS

10 p.m.

LIONKING: welcome back sweetie.

JUNGLECAT: thx your majesty.

LIONKING: tonight we don't talk anything emotional but jokes only.

JUNGLECAT: ist u.

LIONKING: tell me who is she?

She will never stand him up and never let him down. She will reassure him when he feels insecure and comfort him after a bad day.

She will inspire him to do things he never thought he could do; to live without fear and forget regret.

She will enable him to express his deepest emotions and give in to his most intimate desires.

She will make sure he always feels as though he's the most handsome man in the room and will enable him to be the most confident, sexy, seductive and invincible...

JUNGLECAT: it is me, your best friend.

LIONKING: thx but it is whiskey.

JUNGLECAT: lol. we r sitting together in a room, how much u bet if I prove u r not there.

LIONKING: a sweet kiss.

JUNGLECAT: ok. r u there with me?

LIONKING: yes. right in front of u.

JUNGLECAT: but I cant c u. u r not in MUMBAI?

LIONKING: no.

JUNGLECAT: u r not in NEW YORK?

LIONKING: no.

JUNGLECAT: u r not in LONDON?

LIONKING: no.

JUNGLECAT: then u r somewhere else?

LIONKING: yes.

JUNGLECAT: if u r somewhere else, u cant be here. Proved. now give me a sweet kiss.

LIONKING: but I am not here.

JUNGLECAT: lol. u r too smart.

LIONKING: lol. and u say I am stupid.

JUNGLECAT: I can prove that.

LIONKING: prove.

JUNGLECAT: what r u doing?

LIONKING: of course chatting with u.

JUNGLECAT: one who answers a stupid question is a stupid himself. Proved.

LIONKING: but that means u r also stupid.

JUNGLECAT: yes, I am a licensed idiot.

LIONKING: lol. don't ever cancel your license.

JUNGLECAT: most men stare at which body part of a woman?

her face; her butts or her boobs

LIONKING: her face.

JUNGLECAT: no I think it is the boobs.

LIONKING: how can u say that?

JUNGLECAT: I am a girl and I have noticed it a number of times.

LIONKING: does the girls feel pleased when guys stare at their boobs.

JUNGLECAT: may be yes, may be not. not sure.

LIONKING: it is yes bcz that is why they put them on show by wearing push up bras, padded bras to make them look bigger and low cut tops to show them off.

JUNGLECAT: may be u r right. what do u stare at?

LIONKING: I also stare at boobs. bcz since childhood I am fond of fresh milk.

JUNGLECAT: lol.

LIONKING: what do ladies stare at?

Height, face, physique

JUNGLECAT: physique.

LIONKING: I think u r right.

JUNGLECAT: but I look at the face. face expressions r true mirror of one's feelings & thoughts.

LIONKING: when a man and a woman r about to have sex, woman will look at which part of man's body?

  Face, chest or genitals

JUNGLECAT: how can I tell? I have never been through such a situation.

JUNGLECAT: u tell me what a man looks at?

Face, boobs or genitals

LIONKING: I also don't have any experience. But I suppose face & eyes.

JUNGLECAT: why face ? why not boobs?

LIONKING: bcz they look more enticing when they are imprisoned.

JUNGLECAT: lol. what is it that a girl has before marriage but values it only after marrying?

Virginity, freedom or parents' house

LIONKING: Virginity.

JUNGLECAT: no it is her freedom. virginity can be lost even before marriage.

LIONKING: and what is it in case of men?

freedom, wealth or sleep

JUNGLECAT: I think it is freedom in case of men also.

LIONKING: partly right. bcz they lose everything after marriage. lol

JUNGLECAT: lol. why is it so?

LIONKING: it is bcz women r very possessive and they start controlling every aspect of their life.

JUNGLECAT: what about tomorrow?

LIONKING: it will be another day.

JUNGLECAT: a new day.

LIONKING: yes. and it will be renamed as today.

JUNGLECAT: right.

LIONKING: I get it and u also remember it.

JUNGLECAT: let it bring a new light in our lives.

LIONKING: it will. Bye for today.

JUNGLECAT: bye. good night. and sweet dreams.

LIONKING: bye. good night. sleep well and take care.

4 March

The day passed without any incident. I did not pay any notice to Meeta in the college and returned home early for a predinner session of chatting with Radha. I was online at 5.30 p.m., and Radha was there waiting for me.

LIONKING: Hi cattie.

JUNGLECAT: hi king of the jungle. my regards.

LIONKING: r u comfortable and happy.

JUNGLECAT: yes my Lord.

LIONKING: any new development.

JUNGLECAT: nothing.

LIONKING: when one does not know what it is, then it is something, but when one knows what it is, then it is nothing?

JUNGLECAT: now I know the whats and whys and even ifs, so now I feel it is nothing.

LIONKING: idiot. I have asked u a question and u r to answer it.

JUNGLECAT: relationship?

LIONKING: it is a riddle. here is another one

Pronounced as one letter

And written with three,

Two letters there are,

And two only in me.

I am double, I am single,

I am black, blue, and gray,

I am read from both ends,

And the same either way.

What am I?

JUNGLECAT: let me think yaar [friend]. It is a long one. Yes. it is eye.

LIONKING: how did u find out?

JUNGLECAT: starting from A, I eliminated B, C ....and found I (eye) met the conditions.

LIONKING: smart.

JUNGLECAT: and u think I am an idiot. here is one 4 u.

It is greater than God and more evil than the devil. The poor have it, the rich need it and if you eat it you'll die. What is it?

LIONKING: it is greater than God, but nothing is greater than God, it is more evil than devil but there is nothing more evil than devil, poor have it but poor have nothing, rich need it but rich need nothing and if we eat nothing we will die. It is NOTHING.

JUNGLECAT: intelligent and I thought u were stupid.

LIONKING: 4 u I am still stupid.

LIONKING: here is one 4 an idiot like u.

How can u drop a raw egg on a concrete floor without breaking it ?

JUNGLECAT: wrapped in thick layer of cotton.

LIONKING: idiot u drop it anyway the concrete floor will not break.

JUNGLECAT: lol. I have some assignment to do. we will meet again at 10.00 PM. Cu.

LIONKING: cu.

10 p.m.

JUNGLECAT: hi mr. intelligent.

LIONKING: hi miss idiot.

JUNGLECAT: Ashu I am facing problem with this exercise. Can u help me solving it?

LIONKING: I can try. send it via e-mail.

I received the email, and it took me fifteen minutes to solve the problem, and I sent the solution back via email.

LIONKING: solved and sent back.

JUNGLECAT: good. u r intelligent my stupid friend.

LIONKING: my reward.

JUNGLECAT: puchhhhhhhhhhhhh.

LIONKING: ty. Sooooooo sweet.

JUNGLECAT: now I have to go as I have to do the assignment.

LIONKING: ok. good night.

JUNGLECAT: good night. cu tomorrow.

9

LIONKING IN LOVE

12 May 2002

Days passed. Weeks passed. With every passing day our relation grew stronger. We were now chatting in double shifts. Joking, solving puzzles and riddles, discussing studies, exchanging notes on family members, friends, and relatives. My time was divided among studies, NGO work, and Radha.

Radha was occupying my mind all the time. Day, night, I was thinking or dreaming about Radha. I had a feeling that I was in love, but I was reluctant to admit it even to myself for fear of losing a very dear friend. I did not want to break the vow of friendship I had taken with Radha. But I knew I won't be able to hide my love for her for long. But for the time being, I was happy with our relationship.

Nothing important happened during this period. The NGO work was progressing as per schedule. We had covered the interstate bus terminal, the railway station, most of the educational institutions and shopping plaza in sector 17, and now we shall be covering the sectors after the examinations. Membership was increasing, and donations were also coming. But as the examinations were very near, we had put the NGO work on hold.

My examinations were starting from 21 May and Radha's from 23 May. So we were very busy in studies, and now we were chatting for shorter periods.

10 p.m.

LIONKING: hello. How r u?

JUNGLECAT: hello. something happened today.

LIONKING: what?

JUNGLECAT: today it was farewell party in the college and I went to the party wearing a Sari.

LIONKING: idiot. was it intentional?

JUNGLECAT: yes it was knowingly. I wanted AbhI to know the truth.

LIONKING: but why?

JUNGLECAT: I don't know but I had to tell him the truth.

LIONKING: what happened?

JUNGLECAT: he saw what I wanted to show him and he was standing there staring at my belly open mouthed. Then he approached me and asked why I did it and I told him the truth.

LIONKING: he must have abused me.

JUNGLECAT: no. he only asked me to come back and forget everything else. but I told him he had failed the test of love and I was no longer interested in him. That was it.

LIONKING: do u think it was necessary?

JUNGLECAT: yes, I had to do it so that he would stop blaming me for cheating him.

LIONKING: wont he bother u in future?

JUNGLECAT: I don't think he will dare to pursue it further.

LIONKING: let us hope so. incidentally I also met Meeta.

JUNGLECAT: then?

LIONKING: she told me she was getting engaged after the exams.

JUNGLECAT: really. who is the guy?

LIONKING: some software engineer settled in States. after marriage she would also be moving to States.

JUNGLECAT: good for both of u.

LIONKING: I wished her good luck 4 the exams and the marriage.

JUNGLECAT: only few days r left 4 the exams, so let us concentrate on studies and forget everything else.

LIONKING: u mean, u would forget me also.

JUNGLECAT: no never. even if I tried I wont be able to.

LIONKING: let us cut short the chatting sessions.

JUNGLECAT: u r right.

LIONKING: let us utilize the chatting sessions as a rest period between studies.

JUNGLECAT: that would be fine.

LIONKING: ok. bye now.

JUNGLECAT: bye. good night.

LIONKING: good night. luv u.

JUNGLECAT: luv u.

2 June 2002

The examinations were over, and I felt as if a great burden had lifted from my head. It was a Sunday, and I got up quite late. When I went downstairs, everybody was on the breakfast table. I also joined.

Papa: Relaxed? How did you fare in the examinations?

Me: Very good, Papa.

Papa: Now what is the schedule?

Me: Nothing particular. Have to catch up with the pending NGO work.

Papa: What about future plans?

Mom: Let him relax for a few days, then we can discuss about the future.

Papa: Ashu, why don't you go to some hill station for a few days with your friends?

Me: That is not a bad idea, but I have not thought of anything yet.

Papa: Yesterday I received a call from Mr Rohit of Aggarwal Shadi.Com. He has some very good proposals for you from reputed Aggarwal families.

Mom: Ask him to send the details with photographs.

Sonali: Let me make it clear. It will be me who will choose the girl for Ashu bhaiya.

Papa: What if Ashu rejects your choice?

Sonali: Then he will remain a bachelor all his life.

At this everybody burst out laughing. Now discussions about my marriage had become a routine in the family. Aggarwal Shadi.Com sent three or four proposals, but before I could express my views, Sonali rejected them all and nobody could dare to ask her the reasons. I was afraid that if she OK'd some girl, Mom and Papa will be after me for an early marriage. So I took her to a Hindi movie in the evening. I had to take her in confidence. That evening I told everything briefly about my friendship with Radha and how I felt about her.

Sonali: Bhaiya, if you love her, why don't you express it?

Me: Sonali, it is not that easy. We have taken a vow of friendship, and I am afraid that if I express my love to her, she might refuse and accuse me for breaking the promise of friendship, and I might lose a dear and true friend forever.

I took a promise from Sonali that she would not disclose anything to Mom and Papa without my permission. I showed her a picture of Radha, and she liked her very much. Now one thing was certain, that she would not say yes to any of the girls proposed by Mom and Papa.

10 p.m.

As soon as I logged in to YM, Radha pounced upon me.

JUNGLECAT: yahoooooooooo

LIONKING: yahoooooooooooo. very happy.

JUNGLECAT: happy and excited.

LIONKING: why?

JUNGLECAT: the exams r finally over and we r free.

LIONKING: yeah. I am also very excited.

JUNGLECAT: I am coming.

LIONKING: without any stimulation?

JUNGLECAT: how do u know? stupid I am coming to Chandigarh.

I jumped with joy and in the process dropped down the keyboard and was disconnected from YM. Sonali must have heard the sound, and she came into my room and enquired about what happened. I was breathless and told her that Radha was coming to Chandigarh. She was also very excited, and in a single breath, she asked so many questions:

'When?'

'Why?'

'With whom?'

'How long will she stay?'

I told her that I was yet to ask these questions from Radha. I put the keyboard back and reconnected.

'Will you please leave me alone?' I asked Sonali.

'Just a few minutes,' she insisted. 'Let me say hello to bhabhi [sister-in-law].'

'No, nothing of the sort,' I warned her.

But Sonali was Sonali, and she sat down there with me on a chair.

'OK. I will say hello only and nothing more.' She was adamant. I had to agree.

JUNGLECAT: what happened? were u disconnected?

LIONKING: yes, I was so excited that I knocked down the key board.

JUNGLECAT: lol. what would happen when I actually come to Chandigarh? u will not knock me down?

LIONKING: this is Sonali. Hello.

JUNGLECAT: hello. how r u?

LIONKING (Sonali): we r really very excited. when r u coming?

JUNGLECAT: my cousin is getting married on 16th June and we may reach there on 15th June.

LIONKING (Sonali): you will have to stay with us.

JUNGLECAT: Sonali that wont be possible. we will be staying at my Aunt's house, however I promise I shall surely come to meet you all.

LIONKING (Sonali): we r eagerly awaiting the day. now if I don't leave Bhaiya will be angry. good night.

JUNGLECAT: good night Sonali. nice to c u.

Sonali left the room with a naughty smile on her face.

LIONKING: the whole family is coming?

JUNGLECAT: yes.

LIONKING: how r u coming, I mean by train or car?

JUNGLECAT: now cool down. I will let u know the detailed program.

LIONKING: today I told Sonali about our relationship, I mean our friendship and showed her your pic.

JUNGLECAT: what did she say?

LIONKING: I cant tell u. u may not like her opinion about u?

JUNGLECAT: I wont mind. pl tell me.

LIONKING: she said this idiot looking ugly girl is perfect to be my bhabhi?

JUNGLECAT: maroongi [will beat you].

LIONKING: me or Sonali?

JUNGLECAT: of course u. I luv Sonali 4 her comments.

LIONKING: hurrah. that means u r ready?

JUNGLECAT: ready 4 what?

LIONKING: to be her bhabhi.

JUNGLECAT: before that u will have to tie the knot with me. r u ready?

LIONKING: me? I am not such a big fool.

JUNGLECAT: am I not suitable 4 you?

LIONKING: u r an idiot. who will tolerate u 4 the whole of life?

JUNGLECAT: if I am idiot u r stupid, u r a fool to refuse my hand.

LIONKING: I still can use my own.

JUNGLECAT: lol. but I was extending a helping hand.

LIONKING: 4 that u r welcome.

JUNGLECAT: but my hand is asleep right now.

LIONKING: lol. jerk it off.

JUNGLECAT: I cant. u do it. lol.

LIONKING: luv u.

JUNGLECAT: me too.

She must be joking. So it would be wise to withdraw.

LIONKING: r u serious?

JUNGLECAT: I was joking.

LIONKING: me too. we cant break the vow of friendship.

JUNGLECAT: what will happen after we get married?

LIONKING: I did not know.

JUNGLECAT: what?

LIONKING: that we r getting married.

JUNGLECAT: stupid. I meant what will happen to our friendship after we have found our life partners.

LIONKING: we will tell our life partners about our friendship before tying the knot.

JUNGLECAT: yes. we shall remain friends throughout our whole life.

LIONKING: yes, we are inseparable. I cant live without u.

JUNGLECAT: me too.

LIONKING: then let us start living together as friends without getting married.

JUNGLECAT: not a bad idea but our society does not allow it.

LIONKING: then……..

JUNGLECAT: now we r free the whole day. what would be your schedule like?

LIONKING: for this week—sleep, eat and chat with u.

JUNGLECAT: me too. that would be most relaxing.

LIONKING: tomorrow I am getting a mobile phone.

JUNGLECAT: that would be great. we shall be able to talk freely.

LIONKING: 4 that u also need a mobile phone.

JUNGLECAT: what is the cost?

LIONKING: around Rs. 6000.

JUNGLECAT: I have that much money from my personal savings.

LIONKING: so that is a deal. we r buying mobile phones.

JUNGLECAT: now let us call it a day.

LIONKING: tomorrow what time.

JUNGLECAT: starting 10.00 AM.

LIONKING: lol. bye sweetie.

JUNGLECAT: bye. honey.

LIONKING: good night.

JUNGLECAT: good night.

8 June 2002

Very next day, I bought a mobile phone, but it took three to four days for Radha to buy one. Now we were talking freely wherever we were. All useless talk—where are you? What are you doing? What did you have for lunch? What kind of pizza are you ordering? and the like—but we enjoyed talking to each other.

I saw two movies with Sonali and one with the family. I was almost cut off from my friends. Perhaps everybody was relaxing after the examinations. We had again started the Clean Chandigarh project and would now be doing the sectors one by one or two at a time, and the whole of Chandigarh would be covered by September.

Sonali was always enquiring about Radha and pressing me to confess my love to Radha, but I was reluctant and was waiting for the right moment, though jokingly I had expressed my feelings a number of times to Radha, and she had done the same, but we both had dismissed such admissions of love as a joke.

10 June, 9 p.m.

I had started feeling bored while talking on the phone to Radha. Chatting on the net was more enjoyable as we could be more free and frank. I called Radha and asked her to come on YM, and she was immediately online.

JUNGLECAT: hi king of kings.

LIONKING: hi cuttie cattie.

JUNGLECAT: why not on phone?

LIONKING: I enjoy chatting more.

JUNGLECAT: me too.

LIONKING: is the Chandigarh program finalized?

JUNGLECAT: yes. we r coming by car and shall reach Chandigarh by 12.00 noon. we shall stay with my aunt. on 15th June there is Cocktail Dinner in the evening starting 8.00 pm at some hotel. so after lunch I shall be free from 3.00 pm to 7.00 pm.

LIONKING: so from 3.00 pm to 7.00 pm u shall be mine.

JUNGLECAT: stupid my time shall be yours.

LIONKING: we can go anywhere, your parents won't object?

JUNGLECAT: no. I will tell them that u r taking me around to show Chandigarh.

LIONKING: ok. and on 16th June.

JUNGLECAT: there is a small function in the morning and then in the evening there will be Sehra Bandi and wedding.

LIONKING: can I invite you and your family 4 lunch with my family?

JUNGLECAT: u can. I have no objection.

LIONKING: and I know your parents too would have no objection.

JUNGLECAT: how can u say that?

LIONKING: human psychology. prospective son-in-law theory.

JUNGLECAT: have u asked your parents about inviting us?

LIONKING: I will do it tomorrow. but I don't see any problem.

JUNGLECAT: ok then. on 15th sight-seeing and on 16th lunch with your family.

LIONKING: Radha I am sooooooo eager to see u?

JUNGLECAT: have patience. what gift should I bring 4 u?

LIONKING: u r the most prized gift.

JUNGLECAT: u cant keep me with u 4 ever. can u?

LIONKING: if u promise to get your nails cut and your sharp teeth removed.

JUNGLECAT: lol. pl tell me, I am not able to decide.

LIONKING: then bring everything u have in mind.

JUNGLECAT: my pocket does not allow that.

LIONKING: choices?

JUNGLECAT: a watch.

LIONKING: no, that will always remind me about the time whereas I want u to be with me forever.

JUNGLECAT: a shirt? a tie?

LIONKING: no. give me a hankie with your name embroidered in one corner.

JUNGLECAT: how cute. what should I bring 4 Sonali?

LIONKING: bribe? that is a must and a difficult one. let me think, I will let u know tomorrow.

JUNGLECAT: t shirt? ear rings?

LIONKING: yes. small pearl tops.

JUNGLECAT: fine.

LIONKING: I am really excited about taking u around Chandigarh.

JUNGLECAT: I hear sector-17 is a big shopping plaza.

LIONKING: that is right. but don't get any ideas. we will not be going there.

JUNGLECAT: why not?

LIONKING: I am not a fool.

JUNGLECAT: but u r surely mean.

LIONKING: but not as mean as Santa Banta.

Santa told Banta that he saved 50% of the honeymoon expenses by going alone on his honeymoon. Banta said that he saved 100% by sending his wife on honeymoon with someone else.

JUNGLECAT: lol.

LIONKING: I have already bought a few things 4 u.

JUNGLECAT: really. what r these?

LIONKING: multi color bangles.

JUNGLECAT: when we meet u can yourself put them on my wrist.

LIONKING: and what about the bra and panties I have bought 4 u?

JUNGLECAT: u naughty.

LIONKING: lol. do u really want to go 4 shopping?

JUNGLECAT: anywhere u take me.

LIONKING: I can take u shopping but u will be allowed to buy only one thing.

JUNGLECAT: thx. I would rather not go than to buy only one thing. that is not like a lady especially when she is with somebody who is paying 4 the shopping.

LIONKING: lol. I did not say I will pay 4 your shopping. Incidentally I wear designer trousers which don't have any pocket.

JUNGLECAT: miser.

LIONKING: pl don't make a face like that. I will buy u anything u say.

JUNGLECAT: 🙂

LIONKING: that's all.

JUNGLECAT: 😮 .

LIONKING: that's like a nice girl. Soooooo sweet.

JUNGLECAT: ok. bye now.

LIONKING: bye. u have made me hot.

JUNGLECAT: go cool yourself. good night.

LIONKING: good night.

10

JUNGLECAT'S LOVE

Next four days looked like four months. I was very impatient as I intended to express my love to Radha. I was ready to take the risk of losing her, but I could not live like that forever. One day I would have to express my feelings to her; otherwise, I would lose her to someone else. I had a feeling that she also loved me, and she might be suppressing her feelings like me for fear of losing me.

I had already talked to Radha's mom about taking her with me for sightseeing. I was to pick her up at 2 p.m. It was only 11 a.m., and I had already taken two rounds of her aunt's house, but they had not arrived yet. To kill time, I went to the university cafeteria and sat down with a cup of coffee. That was my fourth cup of coffee when I realized that I had not eaten anything since morning, so I ordered one masala dosa. At 1.45 p.m., I got up and proceeded to pick up Radha.

At exactly 2 p.m., I rang the doorbell and was greeted by Radha herself. I paid my respects to her parents, and we left the house in my car. After travelling a few hundred yards, I slowed down the car, and we shook hands and looked in each other's eyes and smiled sweetly.

'Radha, where would you like to go first?' I asked her, breaking the silence.

'I don't know anything about the city. I am all yours, take me anywhere,' she replied sweetly.

'OK. We will first have a round of university. Then Rose Garden, Rock Garden, and then Sukhna Lake,' I informed her like a guide.

'We better go to a peaceful place where we can be alone,' she suggested.

We took a round of the university. I showed her my college from outside, then as we left from the opposite gate, I pointed towards the PGI hospital and then we passed various colleges and Rose Garden, and in fifteen minutes, we were at the Sukhna Lake. I parked the car, and we started walking on the banks of the lake.

I took her hand in mine, and she also responded. We were talking very little, maybe because we were just enjoying each other's company or maybe we both were nervous. Then we sat down on a bench, still holding each other's hand.

'Radha, why are you so silent? Is something wrong?' I asked.

She didn't say anything but looked once in my direction and then diverted her gaze towards the blue waters of the lake where a number of ducks were enjoying the warmth of the afternoon sun. Suddenly I realized that Radha was weeping.

I was very much concerned and took her face in my hands and lovingly asked her, 'What is the matter, Radha?'

'Ashu, I can't hide it anymore. I am in love. I love you from the depths of my heart,' she said with tears still rolling down her eyes.

I was taken aback by her admission of love and let go of her hand. 'Are you joking?' I asked.

'No, Ashu, this is no joke. I really love you,' she said with a choked voice. 'I know I am breaking the vow of friendship and am risking losing a true friend, but I can't help it. I can no longer hide my feelings. It is very suffocating.'

'Radha, you have won. You are more courageous.' I kissed the back of her hand.

'What do you mean?' she enquired with concern in her voice.

'Idiot. You have stolen my words. I myself wanted to say the same.' With these words I opened my arms, and she was clinging to my neck like a small child and was kissing me all over and then we were locked in an embrace for a long time. We were not aware of the looks we were receiving from the passing tourists, and a few of them must have passed some remarks also. We sat there for a long time, looking into each other's eyes. She had stopped crying and was now flashing the most beautiful smile in the world.

We got up and again started walking along the lake. She suddenly pointed towards the lake. There were two ducks and five ducklings playing around.

'Look, Ashu. How beautiful. Look at the ducklings, are not they cute?' she was now coming to her original self.

'Yes, your kittens will be more beautiful than these ducklings,' I teased her.

'Stupid. Not mine but ours.' She was laughing.

'How many?' I again poked her.

'As many as you wish,' she replied with a mischievous laughter.

We sat down on the bank of the lake and started playing with water. We were both having a great time, unaware of the surroundings. We were both wet and again sat down on the bench. I bought a packet of peanuts, and we started feeding each other the peanuts like small kids. Then I whispered into her ear, 'I want a sweet, sweet kiss.'

'You are most welcome. Go ahead.' She turned her face towards me.

'No, not here. People are staring.' I looked into her eyes.

'Who is bothered about the people? Lo, I am coming, let them stop me if they can,' she said with a wink in her eyes.

'Really. A lady's privilege. They can come anywhere.'

And we both burst out laughing.

'Do you want to go for shopping?' I asked her just for courtesy's sake.

'I am not such a fool who would let go of these romantic moments for the sake of shopping. I want to make the most of this precious time. This is not going to come back.' She declined my offer.

'If you remain with me, this time will never go away. Whenever you would be in my arms, the time will stop,' I said romantically.

And this romantic conversation went on and on. We were not aware of the time. I had to drop her back by 6 p.m., and it was already 6 p.m. We hurriedly got up and proceeded towards my car still holding hands. Once in the car, I took her face in my hands and kissed her lightly on the lips, and she responded back with a very passionate kiss on my lips. After that, both of us fell silent as if by opening the mouth we would lose the sweet taste of each other's lips. If she had come on the lake without kissing, she surely must have come again, and I did not want to disturb her in her moment of pleasure. She had closed her eyes and did not say anything till we reached her destination.

'Thanks, Ashu,' she said as I stopped the car.

'Thanks for what?' I asked.

'For the wonderful taste of your sweet lips,' she said and rushed into the house even forgetting to say bye-bye.

9 p.m.

I was on cloud nine and was floating in air. I went straight to my house and to my room and lay down on the bed. I could still feel Radha's breath and the taste of her rose petals in my mouth. I did not eat anything or even drink water for fear of losing the sweet taste and the fragrance of her breath. Mom called for dinner, but I could hear nothing as I was engrossed in thoughts of Radha.

Then Radha called on the mobile.

'Ashu, I have a problem. I was getting ready for the party, but I can't put on the lipstick,' she said in a tense voice.

'Why?' I asked.

'By putting lipstick, I can't lose the taste of your sweet lips,' she poked.

'I myself have not eaten anything or even I have not drunk water for the same reason,' I said in a serious voice.

'Then what should we do?' she asked.

'You put on the lipstick and I take my dinner and then we meet after the party to refresh the taste,' I chided her.

'That is a great idea but—' and she was disconnected.

After that I tried a number of times, but her mobile was switched off. For a moment I thought of going to the party venue and call her outside, but then I decided against it for fear of accidentally facing her parents. Anyway we were meeting the next day at lunch. I took my dinner and lay down on the bed but was unable to sleep. At 11.50 p.m., my mobile started ringing, and I immediately picked it up.

'Where are you?' It was Radha. 'I am looking for you outside the hotel.'

'Idiot. You believed that I would take the risk,' I replied.

'What about the kiss? This is deception,' she complained.

'Tomorrow, darling. As many as you are able to digest,' I promised.

'Do too many cause digestion problem?' She laughed.

'Yes, because they are too sweet.' I laughed back.

'Bye now. Good night. See you tomorrow,' she said in a hurry.

'Bye. Good night.' I realized the phone was already disconnected.

I could not sleep the whole night and kept on changing sides. I was eagerly waiting for the morning. I got up early and, after refreshing myself, gave a call to Radha. She did not pick up, might be she was still asleep. I went downstairs and asked Mom for a cup of tea. She made tea for both of us and sat down with me.

'Ashu, you seem to be very excited? What is the matter?' she asked. I knew she knew the reason, but even then she wanted to hear it from me.

'Mom, I am very happy and excited because of Radha's visit. Mom, I am confessing to you that the friendship has grown into love. Mom, I love Radha very much,' I replied looking into her eyes for a reaction.

'Really, son? I am very pleased and excited. Should I tell your papa?' she asked with a smile.

'Mom, I think we should inform Papa only after the Malhotras' visit,' I suggested. 'Mom, Papa won't object to the relation?'

'He should not. He should be pleased with your choice,' she suggested.

'But, Mom, you have not yet seen Radha. How can you say that?' I enquired.

'Son, I am your mom and in charge of this home. I keep watch on every activity. Incidentally, Sonali has already shown me Radha's picture on your PC,' she admitted.

'Mom, I think we should discuss the matter in the family after the Malhotras' visit,' I suggested.

'You are right. Now get ready and go to the market, I need a few grocery items.' She got up and went to the kitchen.

At around 11.30 a.m., I called Radha and asked her whether I should come to pick them up or they would come on their own, and she informed me they are leaving in a few minutes. I had put on a black suit with grey tie. As I came out of my room, I met Sonali, and I thanked her for taking Mom into confidence and told her about yesterday's happenings. She was jumping with joy, and I had to cool her down and warned her not to say anything in the presence of the Malhotras.

They arrived at 12.15 p.m., and after the exchange of pleasantries, we all settled in the drawing room where snacks and tea were served. Soon we separated into groups. Papa was in deep conversation with Mr Malhotra. Mom was exchanging notes with Mrs Malhotra. Me, Radha, and Sonali excused ourselves and went upstairs. Sonali was not leaving us alone.

'Bhabhi, how do you like Chandigarh?' Sonali intentionally called Radha bhabhi (sister-in-law).

'Bhabhi?' Radha exclaimed turning red in the face.

'Do you mind my calling you bhabhi?' Sonali asked mischievously.

'You naughty. It is your choice, I have no objection. But take care when we are with the parents,' Radha warned with a laugh.

'If you have any objection, no problem I will select someone else,' she poked Radha.

'Chal bhaag [go away].' Radha again laughed.

'So that you two can be alone. Nahi jaoongi [I will not go]. I can go on one condition.' Sonali looked at me.

'What is your demand?' I asked her.

'A kiss from Radha bhabhi on the left cheek and a kiss from you on the right cheek, both simultaneously,' she demanded.

Though we understood her intentions, we obliged as we also wanted the same. As we kissed her as demanded by her, she withdrew and gave a push to our heads and ran away, and we got what we wanted. Our lips touched, and I immediately kissed her and she responded. But it was a short one for fear of anybody coming. We sat there for a long time, looking into each other's eyes. We were silent, but our eyes were doing the talking.

Sonali came and informed us that lunch was ready, and we came down and settled on the dining table. During lunch, only Papa and Mr Malhotra were talking, and everybody else was silent. After lunch, we again settled in the drawing room.

'Ashu, we shall be very pleased if you attend today's party along with your parents,' Radha's mom extended the invitation.

'Mrs Malhotra, Ashu will come, if he wishes. You will please excuse us,' Mom politely declined the invitation.

'Auntie, you will excuse me too. I won't have any acquaintance there and that would mean Radha escorting me all the time and miss all the fun. Further, people might ask questions which could be awkward to answer,' I politely replied.

Everybody nodded in agreement. The Malhotras thanked Mom for the delicious food and invited us to Delhi. Mom gave Radha an envelope containing some cash as a token of her love and then they left.

'Nice people. Radha is very beautiful and cultured,' Mom said in approval, and Papa simply nodded and retired to his room for afternoon siesta.

Me and Mom exchanged glances, and she nodded as if to say everything would be fine. I also went to my room and lay down for some relaxation and fell asleep.

I was awakened by the ringing of the mobile phone.

'Hi, sweetheart. Why did you refuse to attend the party?' It was Radha on the other side.

'It would have caused a lot of inconvenience to you,' I replied.

'I would have been happier in your company,' she asserted.

'But what about the awkward questions your relatives would have asked?' I insisted

'No problem there. I would have introduced you as a friend,' she again pleaded.

'If you insist, I can still change my mind,' I relented. Internally I also wanted to be near her.

'So it is final. You are coming. I am informing Mom and Papa that you have agreed on my insistence,' she mused.

'That would be fine. Give me a ring as soon as you reach the venue,' I replied.

'But behave yourself and don't do any mischief,' she advised.

'I am not that stupid. However, I am concerned about your idiocy. Now hang up. I have to get ready. What should I wear?' I asked her.

'Nothing.' She laughed and hung up.

Idiot. I opened the wardrobe and selected a smoke-grey suit and white shirt and maroon tie. I was whistling and getting ready. At 9 p.m., I got Radha's call informing me about their arrival at the venue.

I reached the venue and apprehensively entered the premises. Luckily, I met Mr Malhotra, and he introduced me to some of the relatives. Radha also reached there and shook hands with me and took me away. We looked at each other and smiled. She seemed to be very happy to have me there. She introduced me to her cousins, and soon I was feeling quite relaxed.

'Radha, I am feeling hungry. Let us eat something,' I suggested.

'Please spare me. Let us have pani puri.' She took my arm and led me to the snacks stalls.

We had pani puri and then aloo ki tikki and some other snacks.

'Do you want a drink?' she asked.

'If you accompany me,' I replied.

'I can't. Mom and Papa may notice,' she refused. But I realized she was also interested.

'You wait here. I will bring coke for both of us.' I winked and she nodded.

I brought two glasses of coke mixed with vodka, and we clinked the glasses and said cheers.

We had settled down on a sofa in a secluded corner and were enjoying each other's company when Radha's cousins dragged us to the dance floor. I was a reluctant dancer, but with Radha's encouragement, I also joined the group. A fast Punjabi number was playing, and everybody was dancing with great enthusiasm. Someone offered us a tequila shot and forced us to take one each. The drink showed its effect, and we started dancing with abandon. We were on the dance floor for about one hour and were very tired.

We took a break, and at that very moment, Radha's mom came and took us for dinner. After dinner, I bade good night to the Malhotras and their relatives. Radha came outside to see me off. We both were looking for an opportunity to kiss, but the place was crowded. I sat down in the car, and she came to the window. I turned my face towards her and smacked my lips. She looked around and hurriedly but passionately kissed me and I responded. The time had stopped.

'Good night and sweet dreams.' Radha withdrew from the window.

'Good night, sweetheart. See you.' I started the car and waved to her.

11

THE APPROVALS

17 June 2002

I got up late that morning. The taste of her sweet lips was still with me, and I smiled to myself. I rang up Radha and came to know that they had left Chandigarh at 7 a.m. I refreshed myself and went downstairs. Mom, Papa, and Sonali were discussing something while having breakfast, and they fell silent when I approached.

'How was the party, bhaiya?' Sonali broke the silence.

'Great. Nice people. We danced for a long time,' I replied.

'Is Radha a good dancer?' she asked.

'Yes, she is OK. Better than me,' I replied.

'Bhaiya, do you like her?' she pretended.

'What do you mean?' I enquired staring at her.

'I mean she looks perfect to be my bhabhi.' She looked at Papa.

'I also like her. What do you think?' Mom asked Papa.

'Yes, she is a nice girl from a respectable family, but—' Before he could finish, Sonali interfered.

'Papa, no ifs and buts. She is going to be my bhabhi,' Sonali insisted.

'Sonali, you keep quiet. This is a serious matter, so let us hear what your papa has to say.' Mom looked at Papa expectantly. Sonali made a face but kept her mouth shut.

'They do not belong to Aggarwal community. They are Khatries, and I can't allow intercaste marriage,' Papa declared and our faces fell.

'But these days intercaste marriages are very common,' Mom argued.

'I am president of the Aggarwal Sabha [an organization], and I myself can't break the traditions,' Papa argued.

'Papa, if you don't mind, may I say something?' I pleaded.

'Yes, son, say anything. We are discussing something in the family. Everybody is free to say anything,' Papa replied.

'What useful purpose these Sabhas serve? You have Aggarwal Sabha, others have Brahmin Sabha, Gujjar Sabh, Jaat Sabha, and so on. First we have divided the society on the basis of religion and then subdivided it further on the basis of caste. This is spoiling social unity and integrity.' I paused to see the reaction. Papa was listening with full attention.

'This division of society is only serving the vested interests of the politicians. It keeps their vote banks secure, so they never want that the social fabric is strengthened. By dividing the society on the basis of caste or subcaste, you are doing a great damage to the society and the country as it hinders the growth by strengthening old traditions and dogmas and blocking new ideas. It is contrary to the ideas of liberty, unity, and fraternity which are the pillars of a healthy society,' I concluded agitatedly.

Papa looked at me with a fixed gaze and then got up and embraced me and said, 'I am proud of you and your views. If you love the girl, I have no objection to the relation.'

Mom and Sonali jumped with joy. I, on my part, embraced Papa and tears rolled down my eyes. I touched his feet, and he blessed me.

'Has Radha talked to her parents about your relation?' Papa asked.

'Not yet, Papa,' I replied.

'Then ask her to do it as soon as possible. Once she takes approval of her parents, I will call Mr Malhotra to ask for her hand,' Papa declared and left for office.

Both me and Sonali were dancing with joy, and Mom was smiling.

I went to my room and sat down on a chair. This was a great day for me. More than half the battle was won. I was sure Radha's parents won't say no to the proposal. I wanted to share the news with her and was about to call her when I realized that she was still on the way and was with her parents. So I decided to wait till the time she reached home and was alone.

It was 12.30 p.m. and I was about to call Radha when the phone gave a ring, and I immediately picked it up. Surely it was Radha.

'How are you, sweetheart?' she enquired.

'Very bad. Papa has not agreed for our relation,' I teased her.

'Oh no. But why?' she cried.

'He says you have a squint in your left eye,' I again teased.

'He must have been mistaken. Both my eyes are OK. You should have told him that there is nothing like that.' Now she was sobbing.

'Frankly, Radha, on second thoughts, I am myself in doubt. Perhaps he is right,' I kept on teasing her. I could not give her the good news so easily.

'You are teasing me?' She could not believe her ears.

'No, that is the truth. But don't worry. I still love you and will marry you with the squint,' I consoled her.

'What about your parents? Will they accept me?' she was apprehensive.

'They already have.' I laughed.

There was a moment's silence, and then she realized what I had said and she shouted, 'Stupid. I will kill you for that.'

I again laughed. But she continued shouting, 'You almost killed me. I was about to have a heart attack. Never do it again. Now give me the good news.' She relaxed.

'Today morning, we had a discussion on our relation. Sonali started the discussion and wished you could be her bhabhi. Mom endorsed her choice, but Papa had some objection because of different castes, but I was able to convince him. He has asked you to take your parents' approval immediately.' I narrated the whole discussion.

'During our journey, my parents were all praise for your family and you. They seem to like you a lot. So I don't see any problem,' she assured.

'But even then, take their formal approval. After that, my papa will call your dad to ask for your hand for his handsome son,' I informed her.

'I will immediately talk to Mom, and then we shall talk to Papa after he comes back from office. You seem to be in a lot of hurry,' she teased.

'Yes. You have made me crazy with your sweet kisses,' I needled her.

'Mom is calling. I will call you in the evening.' She disconnected the line.

I tried to call Radha at 7 p.m., but she did not respond. She called back at 9 p.m.

'Hurrah', she was very excited, 'they have agreed.'

'Congratulations. Should I ask Papa to call your dad right now?' I was myself very delighted and charged.

'As you wish,' she said.

I went downstairs and informed the family about the good news and handed over the phone to Papa to talk to Radha's dad, and they formally put the stamp on the relation.

'It will be a grand wedding which will be remembered for years to come,' Papa announced excitedly.

'What is in your mind, Papa?' I enquired.

'Everything will be unique, starting with the wedding cards and sweet boxes. The best caterer and decorators from Delhi and Bombay will be hired. More than two thousand guests will be invited,' Papa continued enthusiastically.

'How much will it cost, Papa?' I asked innocently.

'Maybe rupees five million, but I don't care. You are my only son, and this is a once-in-a-lifetime event.' He still sounded very excited.

'So you will waste such a huge amount just for this one day. Papa, remember this wealth has been acquired by you through a lifetime of hard work and now you will waste it just for the sake of false reputation and pride,' I argued.

'Son, this is a small expenditure as compared to my resources, so don't worry. I have a reputation in the society, and I have to maintain it,' Papa assured.

'What purpose will this extravagant wastage of money serve? Ninety per cent of the invitees are reluctant guests who simply come to fulfil their social obligations. If you think you will be praised for the pomp and show, you are mistaken. Instead people will be jealous and get heartburns, and instead of praising, they will be criticizing you.' I tried to make him understand my point.

'Son, in our society, to maintain your position and reputation, you have to go with it. So leave this to me, and go ahead with the preparations.' Papa tried to close the discussion.

'But, Papa, this wastage of wealth can be avoided and put to use for some noble cause like starting a charitable trust for which the whole society will not only praise you but respect you. Papa, you are a prominent and leading member of this society, and people look up to you for guidance, why don't you take the initiative and set an example for others to follow by doing away with this extravagant show of wealth and instead organizing the wedding at a simple ceremony in a temple. Money so saved could be put to some useful charitable purpose,' I stressed.

This seemed to have an impact on Papa, but he was still noncommittal and ended the discussions by asking for time to think.

I called Radha at 10.30 p.m. and informed her about the discussions and asked her to discuss the issue with her parents.

Next morning, we gathered again in the living room over morning tea, and the discussion again started.

'Son, I have seen life more than you and have more experience. But we have a generation gap between us. Our ideas, values, and priorities are different, and I have no hesitation in saying that your generation is more practical and down to earth. You yourself have ideals and values which are noble and revolutionary, and I am proud of you for that.' Papa paused, as everybody was listening to him with rapt attention.

'After considering everything, I have come to the conclusion that your views on wasteful expenditure on lavish weddings are really laudable. Though I may face some criticism in the society, but I will go with you,' he declared and patted me on the back.

'Thank you, Papa, and I assure you that there will be no criticism but praise for you,' I said gratefully.

'One thing more, Papa, no dowry, no cash, no car or furniture or anything else. No gift for me or the family in cash except for a one rupee silver coin as a token. Please make these things clear to Mr Malhotra,' I requested.

'Of course, my son, I am myself against these traditions. But will Mr Malhotra agree to our proposals?' he agreed.

'Why not? If he has any objection, Radha would handle it,' I assured.

During further discussions, it was decided that on coming Sunday, we would be going to Delhi for the ring ceremony. Wedding rituals would be performed at a simple ceremony at Chandigarh in a temple followed by a dinner in the evening for about one hundred people at our house for very close friends and relatives.

Papa called Mr Malhotra and exchanged views on the issues discussed, and he readily agreed. He was rather very pleased with our modern attitude and noble ideas. Then I called Radha and informed her about the decisions, and she was also overjoyed.

12

THE ENGAGEMENT

On Sunday, 23 June 2002, we reached Delhi at 12.30 p.m. We were eight people, our family and my paternal uncle's family. We were warmly received by the Malhotras at their residence. After formal introductions, we all settled in the drawing room and were served tea/coffee and snacks. Radha was looking gorgeous in lemon-coloured Punjabi suit. We exchanged glances and I got up, and kneeling before her, I took her hand in mine and proposed to her.

'Radha, I love you very much. Will you marry me?'

'On one condition,' she responded with a mischievous smile.

'Condition? What condition? I thought our love is beyond any terms and conditions.' I was astonished by her reply and so was everybody else, and everybody was looking at her with surprise.

'That you will keep me happy throughout my life,' she mused, and everybody heaved a sigh of relief.

'I don't promise to keep you happy, but I guarantee one thing, that you will always remain happy with me throughout your life,' I assured her, and everybody applauded.

'Then I happily agree to be your wife.' She laughed, and everybody again applauded and congratulated each other.

Next, Radha's dad put a tilak on my forehead and gave me a silver coin of one rupee as a token of accepting me as their son-in-law. Then Mom gave Radha a sari and a diamond set and blessed her. Sonali and Sakshi took Radha to her room to change into the new sari and jewellery.

Radha came back after half an hour, dressed in the new outfit, a magenta-coloured sari with purple blouse. The diamond set was a perfect match, and her radiant face made her a real beauty queen. We settled on the sofa and exchanged rings to the applause and blessings of everybody present, and thus we were now officially engaged to be married. Everybody was congratulating each other with offering of sweets.

After that, lunch was served amid discussions about the probable wedding date, and it was decided that both sides would consult their respective astrologers or priests and then the most auspicious day would be fixed for the wedding. We were given eleven boxes of sweets as a token of blessings from the Almighty.

We reached Chandigarh quite late at night. We had dinner on the way at a roadside restaurant. Everybody was tired, hence retired to their respective rooms.

Next day, I was able to call Radha only at 11 a.m. and asked her to come on YM.

JUNGLECAT: hi would be hubby.

LIONKING: hi sweet heart.

JUNGLECAT: why don't u call me would be wife.

LIONKING: I don't like that word.

JUNGLECAT: do u have a choice now?

LIONKING: do u know what the word 'wife' means?

JUNGLECAT: of course everybody knows what it means.

LIONKING: it means "without information, fighting every time'.

JUNGLECAT: no it means 'with idiot for ever'.

LIONKING: lol. I hope everybody is happy with yesterday's ceremony.

JUNGLECAT: overjoyed. they r all bowled over by your and your family's simplicity.

LIONKING: yesterday I wanted to kiss you.

JUNGLECAT: who stopped you? now u r entitled to do that freely.

LIONKING: next time we meet I will keep that in mind. what else am I entitled to?

JUNGLECAT: no more. 4 more u will have to ist tie the knot.

LIONKING: I cant wait that long.

JUNGLECAT: use your hand as usual.

LIONKING: that is unfair. your parents have agreed to give your hand to me, then why cant I use your hand now.

JUNGLECAT: I am ready to help. Is it up?

LIONKING: yes it always responds to your meow meow.

JUNGLECAT: lol. u know your roar makes me hot and wet.

LIONKING: promise me u will never fight with me.

JUNGLECAT: r u afraid of my sharp teeth and long nails?

LIONKING: promise.

JUNGLECAT: on one condition. u will make love to me on demand.

LIONKING: agreed. but I have heard ladies r very demanding, how many times a day u will raise the demand.

JUNGLECAT: let me see. Ist before getting up from the bed, 2nd while taking bath, 3rd after breakfast, 4th before lunch, 5th in the afternoon, 6th in the evening, 7th before dinner, 8th after dinner and twice more during the night. I think that will be enough. u will agree I am not as demanding as other ladies.

LIONKING: no u r not at all demanding.

JUNGLECAT: lol.

LIONKING: lol.

The chatting and conversations were becoming more and more intimate as the days passed and some of these are not appropriate to be reproduced here.

In consultation with the astrologers, the date for the wedding was fixed for 31 August. So everybody got busier in preparations. I was doubly busy because of marriage preparations and NGO work. I wanted to finish the first round of coverage of Chandigarh before the D-day.

The results for the final semester were out. Mine on 26 June and Radha's on 29 June. Both of us had passed with flying colours, and the families exchanged congratulatory notes. We both were very happy. Though this called for a big celebration, since everybody was busy, we could manage only a small party at her residence during our visit to Delhi on 2 July. But for me and Radha, it proved to be a big party as we were able to steal enough time for a healthy kiss.

4 July

I called Radha at 9.30 p.m.

Radha: Hello.

Me: Hello, darling.

Radha: Hi, sweetheart. How are you feeling?

Me: I can't miss brushing my teeth twice a day. So you have to refresh the taste of your sweet lips every day.

Radha: I will refresh it every hour.

Me: What about your placement with HDFC bank.

Radha: What do you suggest?

Me: I can make you a counter-offer.

Radha: And what is that?

Me: Finance director in Modern Pharmaceuticals Ltd.

Radha: Wow. Accepted without second thought. This way I will remain with you and the family.

Me: That is right.

Radha: Even if you had not made this offer, I had decided to decline the HDFC job. I give priority to family over career.

Me: I am proud of you, darling. How are the preparations for the marriage going on?

Radha: Everything is on the drawing board. Every day we have discussions on various issues.

Me: Now give me a sweet kiss before I go to sleep.

Radha: *puchhhhhhhh.*

Me: *puchhhhhh.*

13

THE WEDDING

We went to Delhi many times for wedding shopping. Radha also joined us when we were to purchase her dresses and jewellery so that we should purchase nothing which did not suit her taste. During those days, we were together for whole days and enjoyed a lot. We even exchanged a few hurried kisses whenever we got the opportunity.

Over the phone, we would discuss all the details of purchases made and other preparations made, and thus the days passed in no time and finally the day, 31 August, had arrived. Radha's family with relatives, twenty-five in number, had arrived the previous evening, and their stay was arranged in Hotel Mountview.

I got ready by 9 a.m. for sehra bandi. I was dressed in a cream-coloured sherwani with matching turban. Sonali tied the sehra on my head, and I gave her a gift of gold necklace set. Then all relatives applied tilak on my forehead and gave me cash gifts.

Radha and her family reached the temple before us. When we reached there at 11 a.m., we were warmly welcomed with a rose for everybody.

Radha was looking stunning in a brick-red sari and bridal make-up and jewellery. She was looking like a deity. I was staring at her with fixed gaze when Sonali nudged me, and reluctantly I had to move my eyes from her. We exchanged glances, and I winked at her and stealthily she also winked back.

Then there was the ritual of *milni* (meeting), which is a sort of introduction of key relatives of both sides.

This was followed by *jai mala* (exchange of garlands between the bride and the groom). Everybody applauded and showered rose petals on us. Then we sat down on the chairs for the *pheras*, and priests lit the fire and started chanting Sanskrit *slokas*. It took more than one hour for the ceremony to finish. In the end, I put *manglasutra* (sacred thread) around her neck and put *sindoor* (red powder) in the front of her hair parting, and we were now legally married. Everybody showered flowers on us and congratulated each other. Then it was time for *vidai* (farewell). Parents and relatives of Radha bade her farewell with moist eyes as she accompanied the *baraat* (marriage party) back to my house.

At home, we were welcomed by Mom, and Radha entered the house after kicking the pot of mustard oil with her right foot, and after that, we took blessings of all the elders present and of my forefathers.

Radha's family arrived after a while, and all of us had lunch together which was served on the back lawn of our house. After lunch, some ritual games like untying the sacred threads, were played between us to the amusement of everybody present there. Then everybody retired to their respective places of stay for taking rest before the evening dinner party.

Radha went with Sonali for changing into more comfortable clothes. I also changed into casuals and took a nap. At 6 p.m., Radha and Sonali left for a beauty parlour to get ready for the party. I supervised the preparations for the party for some time and then went to my room to get ready. I wore a navy-blue suit with white shirt and matching tie. Radha and Sonali were also back by 8 p.m. Radha was looking even more beautiful than in the morning in her light-blue dress.

The guests had started arriving. Mom and Papa were welcoming the guests. Me and Radha were going to each and every guest to seek their blessings. Radha was introduced to all my relatives one by one, and she was quite comfortably conversing with each of them. All the guests presented us with either cash gifts or some piece of jewellery. Then Radha's family and other relatives arrived, and we all gathered to welcome them. I was introduced to Radha's relatives one by one by Mr Malhotra. They also gave us gifts and Shaguns.

Cocktails and whisky was served with choicest snacks. A small orchestra was playing very light music, and a few couples had started moving their feet to the tunes. My relatives and family got introduced to Radha's family and relatives, and now the gathering was divided into small groups enjoying their drinks and the music.

My friends forced me to join them for a drink and forced Radha to have a lemon drink laced with vodka. Radha was very gracious in whatever she was doing, and all eyes were admiringly looking at her, and I was feeling very proud of my love.

Papa along with Mr Malhotra approached the orchestra and took the mike and spoke thus:

'Ladies and gentlemen, may I have your attention please.'

And everybody fell silent.

'Let me first of all welcome you all on this happy occasion. I, along with Mr Malhotra here, am very grateful for your blessings for the newlyweds, Radhika and Ashish. As all of you are aware, this is an intercaste marriage. I am president of the Aggarwal Sabha and wanted to marry my son into an Aggarwal family, hence I was initially against this match. But my son convinced me with his arguments that I was wrong. By forming these Sabhas and societies based on caste or subcastes we are not doing any good for the society and the country. On the contrary, we are damaging the fabric of unity of the social system. If we are really interested in doing some social service, we should do it for the whole society and not for a particular section of the society. Hence I have resigned from the presidentship and membership of the Aggarwal Sabha.'

There was all round applause. Papa continued:

'We, Mr Malhotra and I, were planning to organize the marriage on a lavish scale. But my son and my daughter-in-law considered this extravagant show of wealth a wastage. Millions of our hard-earned money goes down the drain just for the sake of a one-day show, which serves no personal or social purpose. If instead this money is used for some social charity, it can benefit thousands of people. So not caring for the criticism and resentment which we may face from those who have not been invited to this select gathering of a very few close friends and relatives, we agreed to the demand of our children for a simple wedding. This younger generation has dynamic ideas which are more progressive and practical.' Papa again paused and looked around for approval.

'The money saved this way is being put to a social cause. We are forming a charitable trust in the name of my daughter-in-law, Radha Charitable Trust, with the purpose of providing financial assistance to brilliant students who come from economically weaker sections of the society and can't pursue higher studies because of financial constraints. I am contributing rupees four million to this trust.'

There was a long applause from the gathering.

'Further, I am donating rupees five lakhs to Green Ideas Society, an NGO started by my son for preserving the environment.'

Again there was a big applause.

'I am donating rupees one lakh each to the School for Blind, School for Deaf and Dumb, Vridh Ashram [home for old], Bal Sadan [orphanage], and Society for Care of Animals.

'I once again thank you all for sparing time to bless the newlyweds.'

With these words, he handed over the mike to Mr Malhotra. Everyone present was again applauding and congratulating Papa.

Mr Malhotra took the mike. 'I feel really very lucky to have entered into relationship with the Aggarwal family. I appreciate their simplicity and high values. Mr Aggarwal is a very noble person. He has not taken any dowry either in cash or in kind except for a one rupee silver coin. I am proud to have Ashish as my son-in-law. He has high values, progressive vision, and revolutionary ideas which I am sure he has inherited from his parents. Following in the footsteps of Mr Aggarwal, I announce a contribution of rupees two million to the Radha Charitable Trust. May God bless the newlywed couple. I, on behalf of my family, thank you all for joining us this evening on this happy occasion.'

Again there was big applause.

Then both the families gathered around the champagne table. Both Papa and Mr Malhotra took a bottle each and uncorked the bottles and filled the glasses. There was a big applause. Everybody was served a glass of champagne, including me and Radha. We clinked the glasses and so did everybody else, and the party began again.

For the next few minutes, everybody was congratulating and appreciating Papa and Mr Malhotra.

The merrymaking and dancing continued for the next one hour. Me and Radha also danced for a while. Then at 11 p.m., dinner was announced, and one by one, the guests proceeded to the dining tables.

After dinner, the guests started leaving. Each family was given a box of sweets and a small silver statue of Radha and Lord Krishna as a souvenir. The guests were seen off at the gate by both the families. After everybody else had left; the Malhotras also left for their hotel.

14

THE FIRST NIGHT

Sonali took Radha to our room which was decorated with flowers for the *suhag raat* (first night). Radha changed into a nightdress. When I reached there, Sonali was still there. I also changed into a night suit and waited for Sonali to leave, but she did not seem to be in a mood to leave us alone.

'Sonali, we are tired and want to rest. So will you please leave us alone,' I pleaded.

She extended her hand. 'Bribe.'

I took out whatever cash I had in my pocket and gave it to her, and she left after bidding good night to both of us. I bolted the door and looked at Radha who was now sitting on the bed. She looked like a fairy in her nightdress. There was a knock on the door, and I opened it to find Sonali again, but I did not let her come in.

'What now?' I asked in a sharp voice.

'Bhaiya, don't bother bhabhi too much.' She laughed and ran away.

I again closed the door and moved towards the beauty. I was already beginning to have a hard on. I beckoned Radha to come near me, and she obliged, and soon we were locked in a tight embrace with our lips locked. I don't remember how long it lasted. It must have been more than one hour. Both of us were now on fire. We moved onto the bed and lay down side by side. I started removing her nightdress, which she did not resist. She was now only in panties, red-coloured laced panties. When I tried to remove them, Radha held my hand and stopped me from doing so.

'My first night gift?' she demanded.

I opened the side drawer of the bed and took out a box and handed it over to her. She opened it. It was a multi-threaded pearl necklace with matching earrings.

'Wow. It is very beautiful. Thank you.' She was delighted.

I again tried to remove her panties, but she again resisted.

'What is the matter now?' I asked puzzled.

'Have you not noticed the colour of my panties?' she asked teasingly.

'Yes, I have. Beautiful red-coloured panties,' I replied.

'Don't you know what the red colour indicates?' she teased me further.

'What?' I asked hoping against hope.

'*No entry,*' she announced.

'Oh no,' I sighed.

'Oh yes' she mused.

'KLPD*,' I said dejectedly.

'Stupid,' she said.

'Idiot,' I shot back.

And we both burst out laughing.

---

*   For full meaning of KLPD, search the Internet

EPILOGUE

The next day's newspapers were full of praise for Papa for celebrating the wedding of his son in a simple way and putting the money so saved to social charity.

Next week, we left on honeymoon for Europe for twenty days. On return, I joined Modern Pharmaceuticals as director marketing and Radha as director finance.

After two years, I left for USA for a one-year advanced diploma in pharmaceutical marketing. In my absence, Radha looked after the NGO work and started a new NGO, SHE EQUALS HE, for empowerment of the women.

After my return, we modernized our manufacturing units and started a new export-oriented unit and entered overseas markets in a big way.

Abhi got into Indian Civil Services in general quota and is happily married to another IAS officer. Meeta got married to a software engineer and is well settled in USA.

Radha has produced two beautiful kittens. The elder, a boy, is seven years old, and the younger, a girl, is four years old.

Sonali became a doctor and is happily married to a cardiologist in Delhi.

Radha has proved to be a perfect wife, a respectful daughter-in-law, a loving sister-in-law, and a caring mother. *Long live the JUNGLECAT.*